W9-BII-376

SATELLITE SAM
VOLUME ONE:
THE LONESOME DEATH OF SATELLITE SAM

WRITER **MATT FRACTION**

ARTIST **HOWARD CHAYKIN**

LETTERING & LOGO **KEN BRUZENAK**

DIGITAL PRODUCTION **JED DOUGHERTY**

COVER COLORIST **JESUS ABURTOV**

DESIGNER **DREW GILL**

EDITOR **THOMAS K**

SATELLITE SAM

1: THE BIG FADE OUT

"If it's 3:45 and you've dialed up LeMonde, then it must be time for...

SATELLIIIIIIIITE SAM!

Right after this important message from our sponsors..."

GO THREE.
NINETY BACK.
chht.
THREE.
GRID TO ONE, PLEASE.
MIKEY, ANY CHANCE THAT DICK YOU CALL A DAD WILL GRACE US WITH HIS PRESENCE TODAY?
DID NINE JUST BLOW?
WHY THE FUCK IS NINE IN THE DARK?
HE'LL BE HERE. HE'S GOT FOURTEEN MINUTES.
THIRTEEN. IF WE'RE JUST THROWING THE WHOLE GODDAMN SHOW OUT THE WINDOW AND GOING TO PLAN B, I'D LIKE AT LEAST A MINUTE TO GET IT IN PLACE.
CAST TO ONE, PLEASE, AND DON'T KNOCK ANYTHING OVER.
LIBBY, WHERE WE AT?
CALL IT SEVENTY BACK, GIVE OR TAKE.
fiing.

...AND THIS IS THE CONTROL BOOTH, WHERE OUR DIRECTOR DICK DANNING DOES WHAT HE DOES SO WELL...
--OH, GOD DAMN IT. DID YOU NOT SEE THE BIG RED 'ON THE AIR' LIGHT ?
IT MEANS WE'RE MAKING LIVE FUCKING--
--DR. GINSBERG.
AH--HONORED GUESTS.
C'MON IN, WATCH THE SHOW.
I'D INTRODUCE YOU TO EVERYONE, BUT YOU CAN JUST READ THE CREDITS.
THIRTY SECONDS.
WE'LL BE VERY QUIET.
FOLKS, THIS IS GUY ROTH, HE WRITES THE SHOW.
HI.
AND YOU ARE?
CHRIST.
TWENTY.
THESE ARE INVESTORS, GUY.
FOLKS, ONE THING REAL FAST, IT'S GONNA BE ONE OF THOSE DAYS.
YOUR FRIEND AND MINE, OUR STAR CARLYLE WHITE, HASN'T MANAGED TO SHOW UP.
THE GOOD NEWS IS HE'S ONLY IN THE FINAL SCENE, WITH ONE LINE. STRETCH, FOLKS, JUST IN CASE.
GOOD SHOW.
FIVE.

OF ALL THE UNPROFESSIONAL, RIDICULOUS STUNTS THAT NO-TALENT--
HAMILTON, SHH. TRYING TO STUDY.
I DON'T KNOW WHAT THEY TAUGHT IN THAT ITALIAN GYPSY CIRCUS THEY FOUND YOU IN, BUT REAL ACTING CAN'T BE STUDIED.
REAL ACTING DOESN'T HAPPEN IN VELOUR.

HE'S JUST NOT HERE?
HE'LL BE HERE.

HE'S BEEN LATE BEFORE.
HE'LL BE HERE.
CAN YOU SEE MY CROSS STILL?

ONE.
bing!
GIVE ME THREE.
THREE.
chht!

COL. TRUE, WHERE IS SATELLITE SAM?
DEAR, DEAREST NIGHT-SHADE...

...OURS IS NOT TO REASON WHY, YOU SEE. FOR SURELY WHEREVER SATELLITE SAM IS, 'TWILL FALL TO US TO...
CAMERA TWO.
AND I TAKE IT BACK -- SOMEBODY PUT A FUCKING MUZZLE ON HAMILTON, PLEASE.
GO TWO.
CONTROL ROOM
fiing.

JACKIE, DO ME A FAVOR, GRAB A 10K BULB AND BRING IT UP HERE BEFORE THE C-BREAK?
NINE BLEW BETWEEN DRESS AND AIR, AND I'M GONNA CLIMB OUT THERE AND FIX IT.
...BUT WHEN THE STAR POLICE ARE CALLED TO ACT, THEN WE MUST ALL, FOR THE GOOD OF MAN AND...
YOU GOT IT, BOSS.
BETTER THE CROSS THAN THE TATTOO, PARTY GIRL.
MY WORD, HAMILTON DOES GO ON.
OH, TO HELL WITH THIS.
YOU PAY ME TO WRITE IT, NOT WATCH YOU APES SHIT ALL OVER IT--
THAT BIBLE SHIT DON'T FOOL NOBODY, KARA...
ZZZP!
CLINT!

GO ONE.
GUY, YOU WALK OUT OF THIS BOOTH, YOU KEEP GOING OUT THE FUCKING FRONT DOOR AND YOU NEVER COME BACK.
fiing.

GOOD SHOW, SWEET-CHEEKS.
CADET COREY REPORTING FOR DUTY, SIR...

WE'RE TWO FAT ALREADY.
FELLA SPEWS MORE THAN YOSEMITE.
CADET COREY REPORTING FOR DUTY, SIR...
GO TWO.
chht.

EXCELLENT, YOU'RE BOTH HERE NOW. I RECALL-
--WE ARE AWAITING SATELLITE SAM'S RETURN FROM THE OUTERLANDS.
HE IS LATE.

SHOULD WE GO?
WE SHOULD GO.
LIVE TELEVISION.

THREE.
WELL, CHAYEFSKY, WHAT'S IT GONNA BE?
THREE.
fiing.

--WE ARE AWAITING SATELLITE SAM'S RETURN FROM THE OUTERLANDS.
HE IS LATE.
HE HASN'T RETURNED YET?
CONTROL ROOM
ON AIR
SOUND BOOTH
YOU'LL EXCUSE THE SALTY LANGUAGE, BUT CLEARLY TODAY'S A DIFFICULT SHOW--
AW, HEY THERE, DOC.
FREAKIN' RCA LIGHTBULBS, WHATCANYADO?
FOR MIKE.
Umm...
GOOD SHOW.
WE'LL JUST HAVE TO HOPE THAT WHEREVER HE IS... SATELLITE SAM IS SAFE.
BRING DOWN TWO.
ANNND WE'RE INTO C-BREAK.
chht.
CHRIST, WE HAVEN'T BEEN THIS BAD SINCE OUR FIRST MONTH.
FLOOR SET TO TWO, PLEASE.
YOU GOT ANY SPECIAL SECRET IDEAS WHERE--
--I'LL TRY.
THREE IN THE C-BREAK AND I CAN BUY YOU FIVE AT THE SHILL STATION MEANS EIGHT MINUTES--

CARLYLE WHITE. CARLYLE WHITE.
CARLYLE WHITE TO STUDIO ONE, PLEASE.
CARLYLE WHITE TO STUDIO ONE.
HANDSY SON OF A BITCH.

ON AIR
CARLYLE WHITE TO STUDIO ONE.
GANG-WAY!

New York City, 1951.

East 8th
Street.

for Her
The Smart Shop
2J-1215
Astor
Place.

VALENCIA
HOTEL
GREENWICH
LIQUORS
St. Mark's
Place.

OF ALL THE PIECES OF STRANGE YOU'VE NEARLY DERAILED OUR SHOW OVER--
--THIS BETTER BE THE STRANGEST, CARL.
EXIT
Umm--
CARLYLE?
I DON'T WANT TO INTERRUPT ANYTHING, BUT--
--WE'RE ALREADY INTO THE MID-SHOW C-BREAK, AND...

EXIT
Ggk--
--guhh--
--god DAMN IT--
AAIIIIIEEEEEEEEEEEEEEEE
"NOTHING IS GOING TO STOP THE LE MONDE NETWORK, GENTLEMEN.
"I'M NOT SPEAKING TO YOU NOW AS AN EXECUTIVE, BUT AS AN ENGINEER. THIS ISN'T SPECULATION. THIS IS SCIENCE."

THE BEST CAMERAS. THE *BEST*. YOU WANT TO KNOW WHY I'M NOT WORRIED ABOUT RCA? BECAUSE THE "R" STANDS FOR *RADIO*.
OUR CAMERAS FROM THE INSIDE OUT, AND GENTLEMEN, THEY CAPTURE A STRONGER, CRISPER IMAGE BETTER THAN ANYTHING ELSE OUT THERE.
WE'RE GOING TO BE IN FULL COLOR BY 1955. BILL PALEY HAS MURROW. I HAVE EVERY COLOR UNDER THE SUN.
LE MONDE HAS THE BEST SHOWS, THE BEST CAMERAS, THE BEST TALENT.
SATELLITE SUN
LEMONDE
SATELLITE SUN
THE OTHER GUYS ARE GOING TO BE USING THE PONY EXPRESS TO FERRET SUBSTANDARD KINESCOPES COAST TO COAST. AND WE'LL BE ON THE AIR, LIVE, FROM SEA TO SHINING SEA.
YOU STILL NEED TRANSCONTINENTAL CABLE, AND TO GET IT YOU'RE PAYING FOR *RADIO* YOU DON'T *NEED* OR EVEN *HAVE*.
THIS IS TRUE, BUT--
--LOOK--
--WE'LL TAKE GREAT CAMERAS AND FEWER STATIONS RATHER THAN THE OTHER WAY AROUND. I HAVE FAITH IN OUR TECHNOLOGY.
YOU'RE THROWING MONEY AWAY TO LEASE AIR FROM AT&T.
WE'RE *WORKING* WITH AT&T. IT'S THE BEST WAY TO PLAY WITHIN A *BAD SYSTEM*. BUT IT'S ONLY BAD FOR *NOW*.
BY 1954 WE'LL BE IN FOR *TWO MILLION* A YEAR -- THAT'S 15 PERCENT OF AT&T'S ANNUAL INCOME. THEY'LL GIVE US BETTER PACKAGES WHEN WE BUY ALL THEIR CABLE.
IF YOU CAN *AFFORD* TO BUY THEIR CABLE.
WELL...
THAT'S WHY WE'RE HERE, ISN'T IT?

THE FCC FREEZE WILL END ANY DAY-- LITERALLY ANY DAY NOW.
BUT YOU CAN'T BE SURE. SARNOFF-- PALEY-- THEY BUY INFLUENCE IN WASHINGTON.
I'M NOT WORRIED ABOUT WASHINGTON.
YOU SEE, I BELIEVE IN AMERICA. DO YOU?
I BEG YOUR--

AMERICA. DO YOU BELIEVE IN IT?

I WAS IN THE THIRD MARINE DIVISION THAT LANDED AT IWO JIMA AND STAYED FOR A GODDAMN MONTH, YOU--
GOOD, AND THANK YOU FOR YOUR SERVICE, BECAUSE, SEE--

--I CAME OVER HERE ON A BOAT MY MOTHER DIED TO PUT ME ON.
I CAME THROUGH ELLIS ISLAND WITH ONLY MY NAME, A CASE OF LICE, AND A LIFELONG HATRED OF BOATS. AND NOW LOOK AT ME.
LOOK AT US. I BELIEVE IN AMERICA. GOD BLESS IT.
EXCUSE ME...

THEY'RE GOING TO UNFREEZE MORE CHANNELS. LET SARNOFF AND PALEY PAY FOR A HUNDRED THOUSAND LOBBYISTS.
WE HAVE A MAN ON THE COMMITTEE.
AND IN THE END, THE COMMITTEE MEANS MORE BUSINESS. THAT'S THEIR JOB. THE END.
I KNOW THEY'LL OPEN THE AIR-WAVES, AND THEN, WITH YOUR INVESTMENT IN US, WE WILL HAVE AT&T IN OUR POCKETS.
AND CBS AND NBC WILL BE WONDERING WHAT THE HELL JUST HAPPENED.
GENTLEMEN, PLEASE--

--I DON'T THINK YOUR MAN IS BACK YET.

WHAT'S GOING TO HAPPEN?

--MARY MOTHER OF TEN FUCKS YOU GOTTA BE KIDDING ME--
PLACES, EVERYONE. SIXTY- Uh--
--FIFTY EIGHT--
--FIFTY SEVEN--
DICK--
CONTROL ROOM
SOME-BODY LET THE HUMAN-FUCKING-MATTRESS DOWN THERE KNOW TO PAAAAAD!
KEEP US IN THE C-BREAK LONG UNTIL I CUE IT--
DICK--
--GOING TO BE MAKING THIS UP BY SEGMENT'S END--
AND KIDS-- DO YOU LOVE YOUR CREAM OF WHEAT?
I MEAN, DO YOU REALLY LOVE IT?
POP!
Umm--DO YOU LOVE IT A WHOLE BUNCH, WITH ALL OF YOUR HEART?
WHAT-?
I GOT IT.
DICK, I GOT IT. WE GOTTA THROW AWAY TOMORROW AND FRIDAY'S SCRIPTS, BUT--
--CAN YOU RUN THE FINAL SEGMENT WITHOUT MIKEY BEING IN THE BOOTH?

SHIT.
SHIT.
SHIT.
SHIT.
SHIT.
SHIT.
SHIT.
AND KIDS--

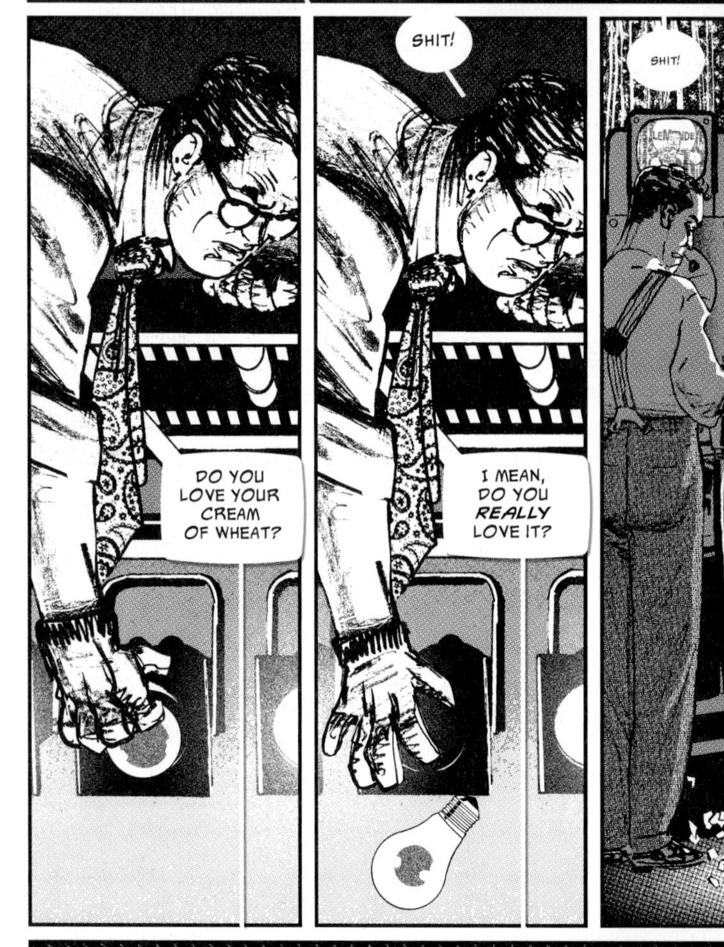
DO YOU LOVE YOUR CREAM OF WHEAT?
SHIT!
I MEAN, DO YOU *REALLY* LOVE IT?

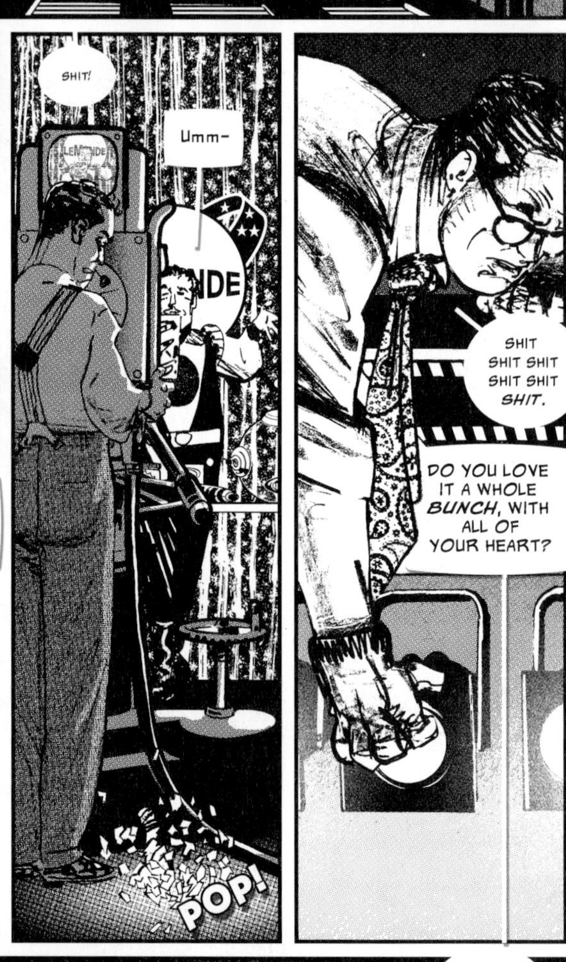
SHIT!
Umm-
POP!
SHIT SHIT SHIT SHIT SHIT *SHIT*.
DO YOU LOVE IT A WHOLE *BUNCH*, WITH ALL OF YOUR HEART?

SHIT.
SHIT.
SHIT.
SHIT.
...YOU AND YOUR OLD MAN...
MIKEY...

...YOU TWO ARE ABOUT THE SAME SIZE, RIGHT?
THROUGH THE CHEST AND SHOULDERS AND SUCH, YEAH?
CONTROL ROOM
ON AIR

IN *THREE* ...
... *TWO* ...

AND GO ONE.
chht.
>hwhark<
"AND...NOW...THE THRILLING CONCLUSION TO TODAY'S EPISODE OF... SATELLIIIIIIIIITE SAMMMMMMM!"
SATELLITE SAM
LEMONDE
SATELLITE SAM
LEMONDE
LEMONDE
NOT DRUNK ENOUGH FOR THIS--
KID COULD STRIP PAINT WITH WHAT HE'S DRINKIN'--
GO TWO.
THREE TO POSITION. IKE, SHUT UP. EVERYBODY, HERE WE GO.
TWO'S UP.
fiing.

THERE--ON THE SPACE RADAR--SOMEONE APPROACHES THE SHIP!
DO YOU THINK IT COULD BE SATELLITE SAM?
YES, I NEED AN AMBULANCE, PLEASE...
IT BETTER BE...
SET RAY-GUNS TO THEIR HIGHEST RADIATION LEVELS, EVERYONE.
AND GET READY TO KILL.
THIS IS THE DUMBEST DAMN IDEA IN THE--
ONE LINE, MIKEY, YOU HAVE ONE LINE.
AND GET READY TO KILL.
Kuh-kuh-kuh-KILL SIR?
WHO KNOWS WHO'S COMING THROUGH THAT DOOR?
CADET COREY, COLONEL TRUE, HOW CAN YOU BE SURE?
WHO KNOWS WHO'S COMING THROUGH THAT DOOR?
I FUCKING HATE YOU ALL.

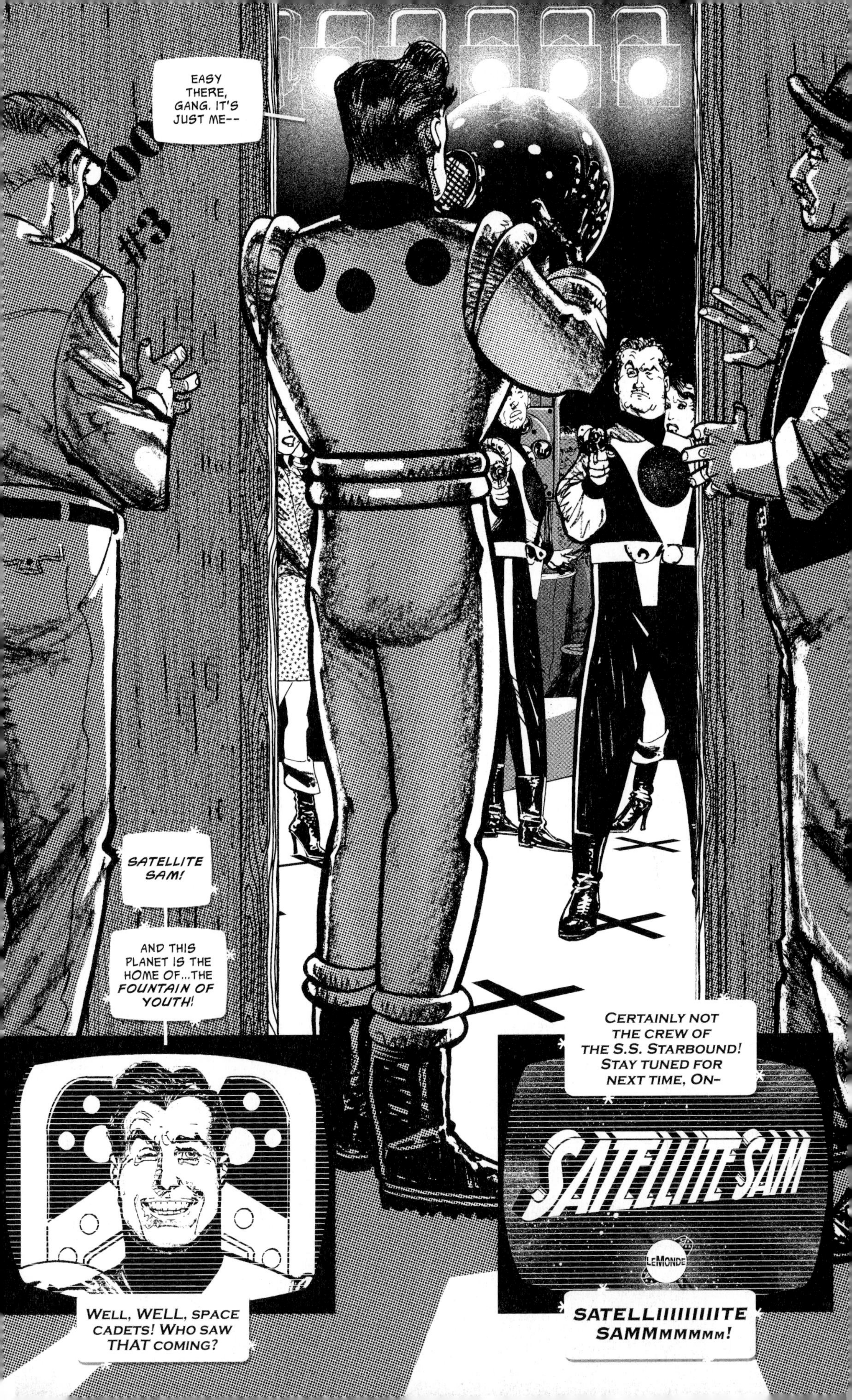

EASY THERE, GANG. IT'S JUST ME--
HOO
#3
SATELLITE SAM!
AND THIS PLANET IS THE HOME OF...THE FOUNTAIN OF YOUTH!
WELL, WELL, SPACE CADETS! WHO SAW THAT COMING?
CERTAINLY NOT THE CREW OF THE S.S. STARBOUND! STAY TUNED FOR NEXT TIME, ON-
SATELLITE SAM
LEMONDE
SATELLIIIIIIIIITE SAMMMMMMM!

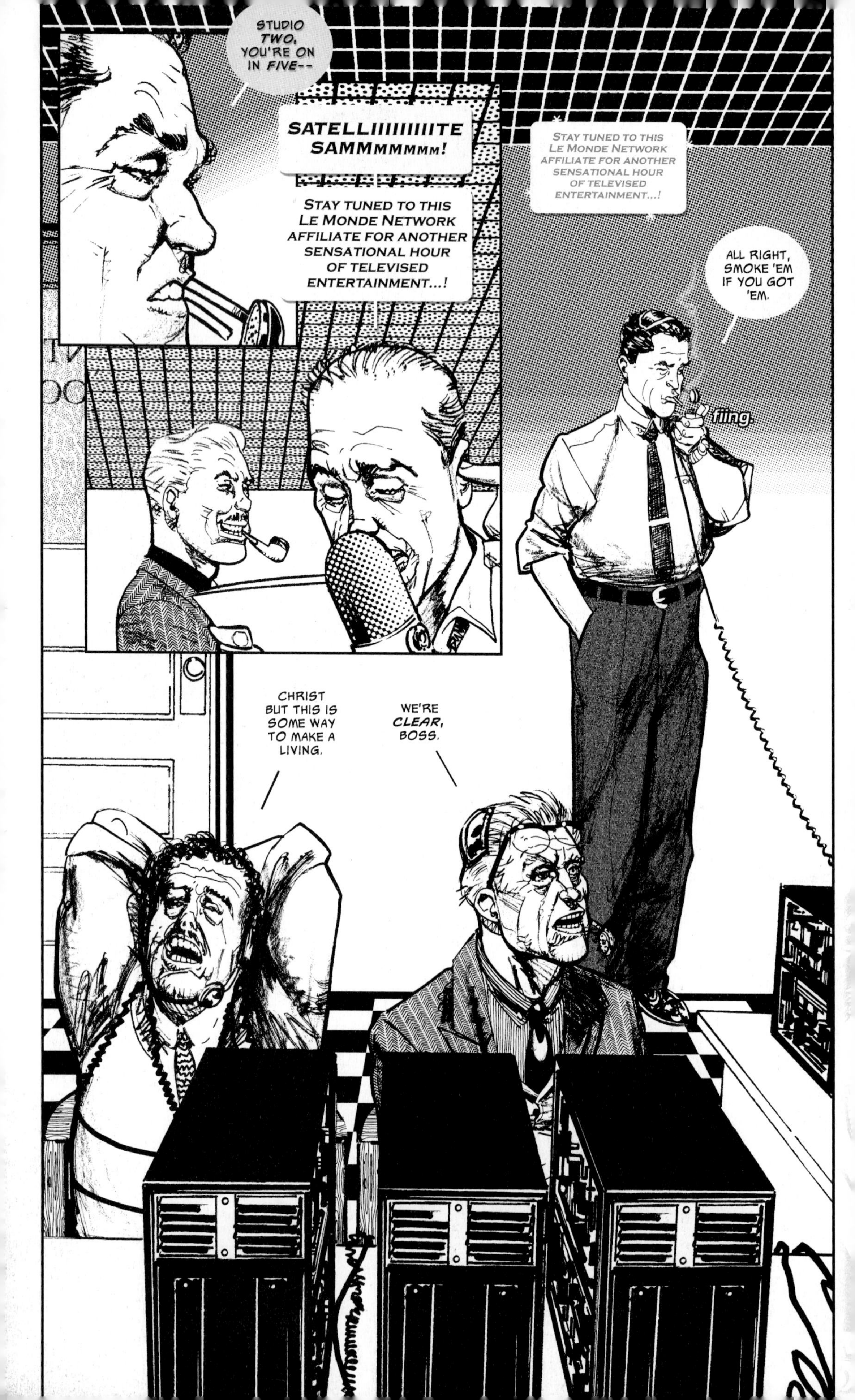
STUDIO TWO, YOU'RE ON IN FIVE--
SATELLIIIIIIIIITE SAMMMMMMM!
STAY TUNED TO THIS LE MONDE NETWORK AFFILIATE FOR ANOTHER SENSATIONAL HOUR OF TELEVISED ENTERTAINMENT...!
STAY TUNED TO THIS LE MONDE NETWORK AFFILIATE FOR ANOTHER SENSATIONAL HOUR OF TELEVISED ENTERTAINMENT...!
ALL RIGHT, SMOKE 'EM IF YOU GOT 'EM.
fiing.
CHRIST BUT THIS IS SOME WAY TO MAKE A LIVING.
WE'RE CLEAR, BOSS.

GREAT JOB, MIKEY--
WHATTA SAVE! WHATTA LOAD OF FUCKING HORSESHIT, BUT WHATTA SAVE.
SO GOOD, MICHAEL, BRAVO.
BLESS YOU. (mwah)
WHO'S BUYING THE FIRST ROUND FOR WE TWO CONQUERING HEROES?

WE'RE LOOKING FOR MICHAEL WHITE.
WE WERE TOLD HE WAS HERE.
BIG FELLA, DOWN THE END THERE.

'SCUSE ME.
PARDON.
Uh-oh.

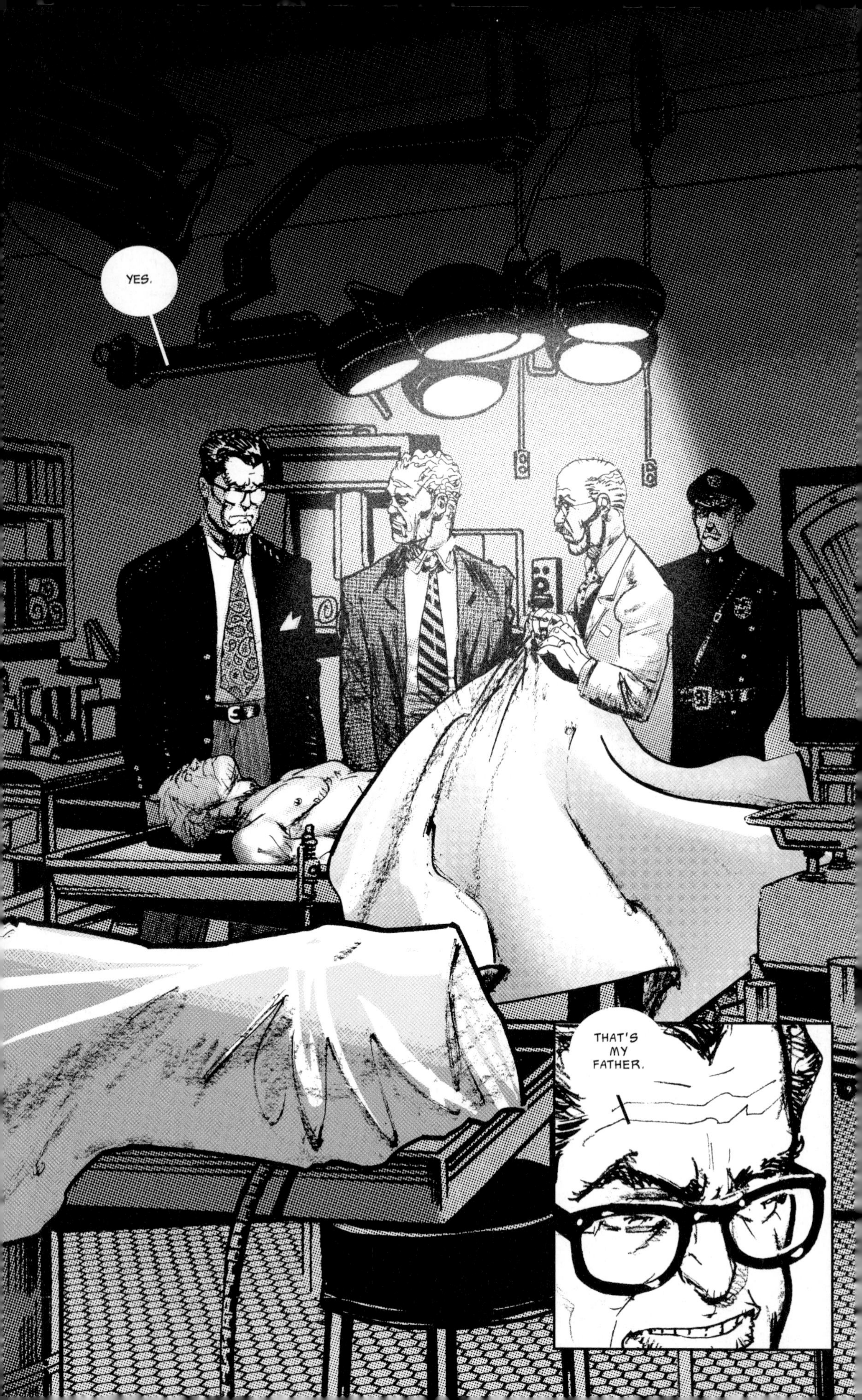
YES.
THAT'S MY FATHER.

THIS... THIS WAS HIS PLACE? YOU'RE SURE?
HIS NAME'S ON THE LEASE, AND THE GIRL, ahh--
--ELIZABETH MEYERS, FROM YOUR NETWORK, FOUND HIM HERE.
LIBBY KNEW. Huh.
WHAT, ahh-
WHAT DO I DO?
WHAT DO YOU MEAN?
NO. THEY'VE TAKEN EVERYTHING THEY NEED. YOU CAN--
THIS... ALL THIS... WHAT IS THIS? ISN'T IT A CRIME SCENE STILL, OR--
--DO I LEAVE IT OR DO I HAVE TO PACK IT UP OR--
BUDDY, I DON'T CARE. YOUR MESS TA CLEAN UP NOW.
OR MAYBE THE SUPER. I DON'T KNOW.
SORRY FOR YOUR LOSS.
GGHAAWWH!

Huhh--
--fuhh--
--HUUGGKK!

WHAT TH--

--LI'L BOXES 'N SHIT...
...WELL FUCK YOUR LITTLE BOXES, DAD, 'N FUCK YOU.

--AW, DAMN IT--
DID HE TAKE ALL OF THESE?
OH, POP.
POP, WHAT THE HELL WERE YOU INTO UP HERE?

SATELLITE SAM

2: THE DIRT NAP

WELL MIKEY? — WHAT DO YOU THINK? —

FUCKIN' CALIFORNIA, RIGHT? C'MON.
RIGHT, MIKE?
HELL YEAH, KID-- C'MON! END OF NEXT YEAR, CONTRACT ENDS, WE MOVE IT OUT HERE.
ALL OF IT. CAST, CREW, SETS. WE'LL GO FIVE GRAND AN EPISODE JUST SHOOTING TO FILM. FUCK IT.
YEAH, POP. YEAH.
FUCK LeMONDE AND GINSBERG AND HIS VIDEO CAMERAS.
THE LOT'S A STEAL AT THIS PRICE. EVER SINCE GOWER WENT OUT OF BUSINESS, IT'S JUST USED AS STUDIO STORAGE.
NO MORE LIVE TV. NO MORE NEW YORK, NO MORE--NO MORE FUCKING ANYTHING, MIKEY. SHOOT TO FILM, DUMP TO TAPE, YOU'RE THE BOSS, APPLESAUCE.
SYNDICATION, CROSS-COUNTRY CO-AX CABLE MEANS TV ANYTIME, ALL THE TIME.

THREE CAMERAS, STUDIO AUDIENCE. FEWER LIGHTS. WE'LL BUY OLD MOVIE CAMERAS FOR A SONG.
KIDS IN CALIFORNIA, KIDS IN MANHATTAN -- ALL WATCHING THE SAME SHOW FROM THE SAME SOURCE --AND WE OWN THE STUDIO.

WE OUGHTA BE IN PICTURES.
AND DON'T EVEN GET ME STARTED ON THE PUSSY OUT HERE.

WAY OF THE FUTURE, MIKEY.

"WAY OF THE FUTURE..."
"WAY OF THE FUTURE..."
"WAY OF THE FUTURE..."
"WAY OF THE FUTURE..."
HHAAUUUUGH!

JESUS CHRIST, JOSEPH, I JUST DON'T UNDERSTAND HOW YOU CAN BE SO CALM ABOUT IT.

SIMPLE, MADELINE.
EVERY MORNING I WAKE UP AND MAKE A LIST OF THINGS I CAN TAKE CARE OF BEFORE RETURNING TO BED...

...AND ALL OF THE THINGS FAR OUTSIDE OF MY ABILITIES TO CHANGE.
THIS IS ONE OF THOSE.

GOOD, MAKE JOKES.
NOW IS ABSOLUTELY THE TIME TO MAKE JOKES.

THE CONVERSATION WILL HAPPEN WHEN THE CONVERSATION HAPPENS.
CARLYLE WAS A STUBBORN AND SELFISH ASSHOLE WHO LET HIS DICK DO HIS THINKING, AND HIS DICK WAS THINKING ABOUT CALIFORNIA BLONDES.
HE'S GONE? Pfft. FINE. BETTER FOR US.

THE ONLY THING MICHAEL THINKS ABOUT IS WHERE HIS NEXT BOTTLE COMES FROM.
MOVING THE SHOW MEANS EFFORT HE DOESN'T HAVE IN HIM.
THE CONVERSATION WILL HAPPEN WHEN IT HAPPENS, MADELINE.

TODAY, LET THE BOY BURY HIS STUBBORN, SELFISH, ASSHOLE FATHER.

"SATELLITE SAM! WE WAITED FOR WHAT SEEMED LIKE HOURS-- DAYS -- FOR YOU TO RETURN!"
"AND I APPRECIATE IT, MAJOR MELINDA--
"--SORRY IT TOOK ME SO LONG."
"OH, SAM, WE'RE JUST HAPPY THAT YOU'RE SAFE."
"WHAT WAS ALL OF THIS RIGAMAROLE ABOUT THE FOUNTAIN OF YOUTH?"
"YEAH, BOSS-- THOUGH I GOTTA SAY YA LOOK ABOUT TEN YEARS YOUNGER!"
"AND I FEEL IT TOO, FELLAS."
"WHAT KIND OF MAGIC MADE THIS POSSIBLE?"
"WELL, I'M NOT THE MAN I USED TO BE. Ha ha.
"I WAS IN PURSUIT OF THE MALDOORIAN DRAGON OF VENUS, FOLLOWING AFTER IT, STAYING OUT OF SIGHT-
"--AND I'M TELLING YOU, I MUST HAVE LOST MY FOOTING, BECAUSE I FELL FROM THE ROCKY MOUNTAIN PATH AND LANDED IN A STRANGE, NASTY, MARSH.
"NOW I FEEL LIKE I COULD LIVE FOREVER."

THAT'S RIGHT, BOSS!
SATELLITE SAM WILL NEVER DIE!

"MICHAEL?"

"MICHAEL?"

MICHAEL, HE'LL SEE YOU NOW.
THANKS, SORRY.
SORRY.

LeMONDE
MIKEY, COME IN. SIT.
SURE THING, DOC.
PLEASE -- JOE, JOE, CALL ME "JOE."
BOURBON NEAT, IF I RECALL?
THAT'LL DO.
PLEASE. LEAST I CAN DO FOR YOU ACCOMMODATING ME DURING THIS TERRIBLE TIME.
BUT IT'S IMPORTANT FOR YOU TO HEAR THIS FROM ME WITH NO MIDDLEMAN OR CANDY-ASS LANGUAGE IN BETWEEN--
--YOU AND SATELLITE SAM ALWAYS HAVE A HOME ON LeMONDE'S AIR, MICHAEL.
YOUR FATHER KNEW IT--
--AND NOW YOU KNOW IT, TOO.
OKAY? OKAY.
YOU CAN STAY ON THE SHOW, YOU CAN MOVE BACK TO THE BOOTH--
--WE'LL FIND A WAY. YOU'RE THE BOSS.
"...APPLESAUCE."
BEG PARDON?
NOTHING. SOMETHING DAD USED TO SAY.
THE SHOW'S CONTRACT WAS UP AT THE END OF THE YEAR, MICHAEL, AS I'M SURE YOU KNOW.
DID HE EVER SPEAK TO YOU ABOUT IT?

...
FUCK IT. FUCK LeMONDE AND GINSBERG AND HIS VIDEO CAMERAS.
THE OLD MAN TENDED TO KEEP HIS OWN COUNSEL ABOUT STUFF LIKE THAT, DOC.
Mmm.
HE HAD GRAND PLANS FOR THE SHOW. WE WERE WORKING OUT BASIC NUMBERS--HIS, YOURS, KEY STAFF. IT'S OUR FLAGSHIP SHOW ON LeMONDE, AND WE WERE TALKING ABOUT A LONG, FRUITFUL RELATIONSHIP.
LEMONDE
YOURS OR YOUR DAD'S?
WELL...
...IT'S MINE NOW.
"I'M TRYING MY GODDAMNDEST TO STOP THE BLEEDING AT MY NETWORK. WHAT DO YOU THINK I'M--"

--AND A LITTLE GOOD NEWS FROM YOU WOULD GO A LONG WAY TOWARDS HELPING ME DO THAT.
BUT, YOU'VE SAID--
--BUT YOU-
--BUT YOU'VE SAID--
I CAN'T GET INVESTORS--
--MY GOLDEN GOOSE DIES--
--AND ALL THE CAMERAS AND SCREENS IN THE WORLD WON'T SAVE ME. IF YOU COULD JUST MAKE GOOD ON ONE OF YOUR GODDAMN PROMISES--
YES, OF COURSE YOU'RE RIGHT. I BEG YOUR PARDON...
...MR. COMMIS-SIONER.
WERE I TO RECEIVE A GUARANTEE THAT THE AIR MY NETWORK NEEDS TO SURVIVE WILL BE MADE AVAILABLE...
...THEN I CAN PROMISE HE'LL STAY. "SATELLITE SAM" AND ITS REVENUE WILL STAY IN NEW YORK WITH LeMONDE.
SAY, WHEN CAN MADDIE AND I GET YOU AND JEANIE OUT TO THE HOUSE AGAIN?
"PRAYER."

THE POWER OF PRAYER. AND I'M NOT TALKING ABOUT ASKING GOD TO MAKE YOUR TRAIN IN THE MORNING, OR THAT BIG RAISE YOU'VE BEEN HOPING FOR.
HOW OFTEN DO WE PRAY--
--REALLY, REALLY PRAY--
--FOR ALL THE OTHER PEOPLE IN OUR LIVES?
Telling His Truth
OF COURSE WE WANT THE BEST FOR OUR FRIENDS, OUR FAMILIES, OUR LOVED ONES.
THINK FOR A MOMENT ABOUT HOW HARD IT IS, THOUGH, TO PRAY FOR, WELL, THE OTHER ONES.
THE GRAINS OF SAND IN OUR LIVES. THE ONES THAT MAYBE STOP OUR JOURNEY FROM BEING SMOOTH.
Telling His Truth
LEMONRE
HOW OFTEN DO WE PRAY FOR THE DIFFICULT ONES? I'VE FOUND THE MORE I PRAY FOR THEM, THE MORE...LOVING A PERSON I BECOME.
BACK TO ONE, PLEASE.
AFTER ALL, IT'S THE GRAIN OF SAND THAT BECOMES A PEARL INSIDE AN OYSTER.
snap
WHERE'S DICK?
RUNDOWN FOR THIS WEEK'S SAM.
AND TWO.
"WHERE ARE WE?"

THE, Ah--THE FUCKING WHAT NOW?
STAFF LOUNGE
THE "MALDOORIAN SAVAGES" HAVE COME OUT OF THE MARSH, AND--
CAN IT BE "A" SAVAGE?
NOT THRILLED ABOUT "OUT OF THE MARSH." MIGHT COULD MANAGE SOMETHING WITH THE TRAPDOOR--
--BUT "FROM BEHIND SOME TREES" WILL SURE AS SHIT WORK EASIER...
OKAY, SO ONE IS A MASTER--
--TO TWO TO FOLLOW THE SAVAGES-OR-SAVAGE, THREE--
--WITH THREE WE'LL PICK UP--
DICK.
A MOMENT OF YOUR TIME.
STAFF LOUNGE
COMING. DOCTOR.

WHY DO ALL OF YOU INSIST ON CALLING ME DOCTOR?
IT'S HOW YOU INTRODUCE YOURSELF TO EVERYBODY YOU MEET, DOC.
HA HA. YES, WELL...
STAFF LOUN

DICK, LOOK-- YOU'RE THE BEST IN THE BUSINESS.
YOU'RE CERTAINLY BETTER THAN *THIS* SHOW...
...BUT RIGHT NOW, WITHOUT CARLYLE, AND WITH MIKEY DEEP-SIXING HIMSELF IN HOOCH MORNING, NOON AND NIGHT...
...YOU'RE THE *GLUE* HOLDING IT TOGETHER.
YOU'RE *KIND,* DOC, BUT I'VE GOT A SHOW TO DO, AND--

DICK, I KNOW EVERYONE'S CONTRACTS ARE UP SOON, BUT I *NEED YOU* HERE. IT'S OUR *MOST PROFITABLE* SHOW. IT KEEPS THE LIGHTS ON.

IF YOU STAY HERE-- YOU KEEP THIS PLACE GLUED TOGETHER A LITTLE WHILE LONGER--
--DICK, WHEN WE'RE COAST-TO-COAST, I'LL BUILD YOU YOUR OWN *PLAYHOUSE 90* AND LET YOU RUN IT, LET YOU STAFF IT. NO MORE DAILY, NO MORE SHILLING FOR SPONSORS IN YOUR SHOW.
DOC...

...I'M A WORKING MAN. HERE. FOR SARNOFF. I DON'T CARE.
YOU WRITE ALL THAT DOWN ON A PIECE OF PAPER AND IT'LL BE *HERE*.

OKAY, WHERE WERE WE?
MARSH SAVAGES.

"WHO THE HELL WRITES THIS SHIT?"
WELL, GOOD MORNING, BOYS. THANKS FOR THE INVITE.
SUSPENSE IS KILLING ME. TO WHAT DO I OWE THE PLEASURE OF THE MEAL?
SURELY IT'S NOT MY SPARKLING WIT AND CONVERSATIONAL BRIO...
IF CARLYLE, GOD REST HIS SOUL, WAS THE CAPTAIN OF THE GOOD SHIP SATELLITE SAM, THEN SURELY YOU ARE ITS RUDDER.
WE JUST-- HAMILTON AND ME--
--WE AIN'T EXACTLY LEADING MEN.
AND SEEING AS HOW OUR INTERIM LEADING MAN KEEPS HIMSELF PICKLED--
--WE'RE THINKIN' MAYBE THERE'S MILEAGE IN THE ADVENTURES OF CADET COREY AND COLONEL TRUE.
THAT PERHAPS ONE COULD RACK FOCUS MORE ON THE SUPPORT STAFF, WITH AN EYE ON--
--THE FUTURE, REALLY. LESS SATELLITE SAM AND MORE--
CONTRACTS ARE UP SOON FOR EVERY-BODY, GUY. OURS, YOURS, EVERYBODY.
WITH NO CARLYLE WHITE THERE'S NO SATELLITE SAM, AND WITH NO SATELLITE SAM...
I'M SORRY, ARE YOU PITCHING ME A FUCKING SHOW?
Menu

Fuh.
FUCK. C'MON.
fipfipfipfipfipfipfipfipfipfipfipfipfipfipfipfipfipfipfipfipfip
Ehn.
Ehn.
FIPFIPFIPFIPFIPfipfipfipfipfipfipfipFIPFIPFIPfipfip
C'MON. COME ON--
--JUST GONNA BE--
--OH, FUCK.
PLEASE.
FUCK.
fipfipFAPFAPFAPfipfip FAP FAP--

FUCK!
FUCK.
...?
FUCK.

IN THE NIGHT, HOUGH WE'RE APART
HERE'S A GHOST OF YOU WITHIN MY HAUNTED HEART
GHOST OF YOU, MY LAST ROMANCE
IPS THAT LAUGH, EYES THAT DANCE

NEVER HAD YOU FIGURED FOR A *JAZZ MAN*, GENE.
WELL, DR. GINSBERG, I'M *NOT* A "JAZZ MAN."

I'M A *PUSSY MAN* --BEST PUSSY'S IN JAZZ CLUBS.

Ah-- YES, WELL.
WELL, I'D IMAGINE.
I, Ah, AS YOU, WELL, YOU KNOW *MRS. GINSBERG* AND--

DOC, I GOT *THINGS* TO...
...WELL, TO *TRY*.
CAN WE GET THE DEAL-WITH-THE-DEVIL PART OF THIS CONVERSATION OUT OF THE WAY?

BEG PARDON?
YOU'RE GOING AROUND.
YOU'RE TALKING TO PEOPLE.
OTHER PEOPLE HEAR AND WORD GETS AROUND--
--ESPECIALLY WHEN NONE OF US KNOW HOW MUCH LONGER WE'LL BE WORKING FOR YOU.
I DON'T KNOW WHAT YOU'VE BEEN HEARING, GENE--
-AND QUITE FRANKLY, I BRISTLE AT THE COMPARISON BETWEEN THE DEVIL AND MYSELF.
I RUN A NETWORK. I RUN SEVERAL PROGRAMS, AND IT IS IN MY BEST INTEREST--
--TO ENSURE THE PEOPLE WORKING ON THESE PROGRAMS HAVE THEIR BEST INTERESTS MET.
AND?
DICK'S OUT AT THE END OF THE YEAR, GENE.
I THOUGHT YOU WERE MY GUY TO RUN SATELLITE SAM.
MIKEY'S IN?
WE WOULDN'T BE HAVING THIS CONVERSATION IF HE WASN'T.
GOOD LUCK CHASING YOUR STRANGE TONIGHT, GENE.

DREAMS ARE DUST
OU WHO MUST BELONG TO...
AND THRILL MY HAUNTED HEART
E STILL MY HAUNTED HEART
CLUB SAMOA
Jimmy RYAN'S
BAR
LEON & EDDIE
BILLY ECKSTINE
JACK TEAGARDEN
CLUB.
DIZZY GILLESPIE
AIR CONDITIONED

Ike Eiger
Guy Roth √
~~Libby Meyers~~
Dick Danning √
Gene Ford ?

LEON AND EDDIE'S
SAVE ME FROM ALL THESE *FUCKING* ARTISTS...
Leon & Eddie's
Air Cooled
Cool and Comfortable
SWING CLUB

"...AND CARLYLE WHITE, I HOPE YOU'RE BURNING IN HELL."

"...AND WHO DO WE DO IT FOR?" NO...
"FOR WHOM DO WE DO THESE THINGS?" OKAY.
KNOCK KNOCK
...YES?

KARA. IT'S MIKE.
MICHAEL WHITE.
SORRY IT'S LATE, BUT I HAVE A QUESTION ABOUT MY DAD--

ONE MOMENT. I CAN--
--MICHAEL!

HOW WELL DID YOU KNOW MY FATHER?

AND TELL THE TRUTH.

I WAS SO...SPIRITED...BACK THEN.

3: PERCHA

DON'T EVEN REMEMBER WHEN I GOT THE TATTOO, OR WHY, JUST...
...ONE DAY, THERE IT WAS.

YOU EVER LOSE TIME, MICHAEL?
START OFF WITH A DRINK AFTER WORK ONE NIGHT AND WAKE UP SOMEWHERE ELSE A FEW DAYS LATER?
I USED TO OFTEN.
BEFORE I FOUND CHRIST, BEFORE I LET THE LORD INTO MY LIFE, I MEAN.

Mm.

I REMEMBER YOU BACK THEN. I REMEMBER WHO YOU WERE WHEN I WENT *OVERSEAS*, AND I SEE WHO YOU ARE NOW.
EVERYONE PRETENDS THAT IT WAS A HUNDRED YEARS AGO, BUT I REMEMBER.

--THOUGHT THISHA FUCKIN' *COWBOY TOWN*, BUT YER ALL NIGGER-LOVIN' *COCK-SUCKERS*--
--SO, C'MON, WHICHA YOU FAGGOTS IS GONNA *FUCK ME*--
GET HER *DOWN*, MIKE--
--NOW.
ON IT, POP...

FUCKIN' FAGGOTS! FUCKIN'--

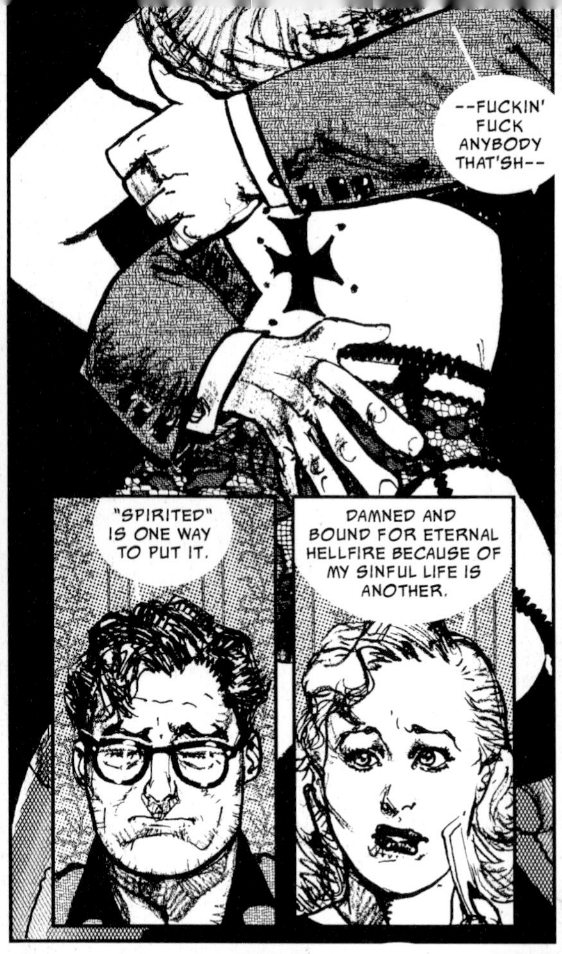
--FUCKIN' FUCK ANYBODY THAT'SH--
"SPIRITED" IS ONE WAY TO PUT IT.
DAMNED AND BOUND FOR ETERNAL HELLFIRE BECAUSE OF MY SINFUL LIFE IS ANOTHER.

Eh, TOMATO, TO-MAHT.
SO WHAT WAS...THERE'S BOXES OF GIRLS, KARA. BOXES.
HE WAS PRETTY SPIRITED, TOO, MICHAEL. THAT CAN'T COME AS A SURPRISE.

THE OLD MAN ALWAYS WAS A COLLECTOR.
HE NEVER SEEMED SENTIMENTAL ABOUT TRIM.

SHIT-
-SORRY-
-I DIDN'T MEAN TO SAY-
RELAX, MICHAEL.
THANK YOU FOR TRYING, AT LEAST. THANK YOU FOR RESPECTING THE IDEA YOU MIGHT OFFEND ME.
AND ANYWAY, I'M AWARE OF WHAT YOUR FATHER AND I WERE TO ONE ANOTHER THEN.

WELL, I'M NOT. AND YOU ARE ONE OF LITERALLY HUNDREDS, KARA.
THE OLD MAN HAD THIS SECRET WORLD HE LIVED IN WHEN NOBODY WAS AROUND.
WHAT WERE YOU TO HIM? WHO WAS MY FATHER?

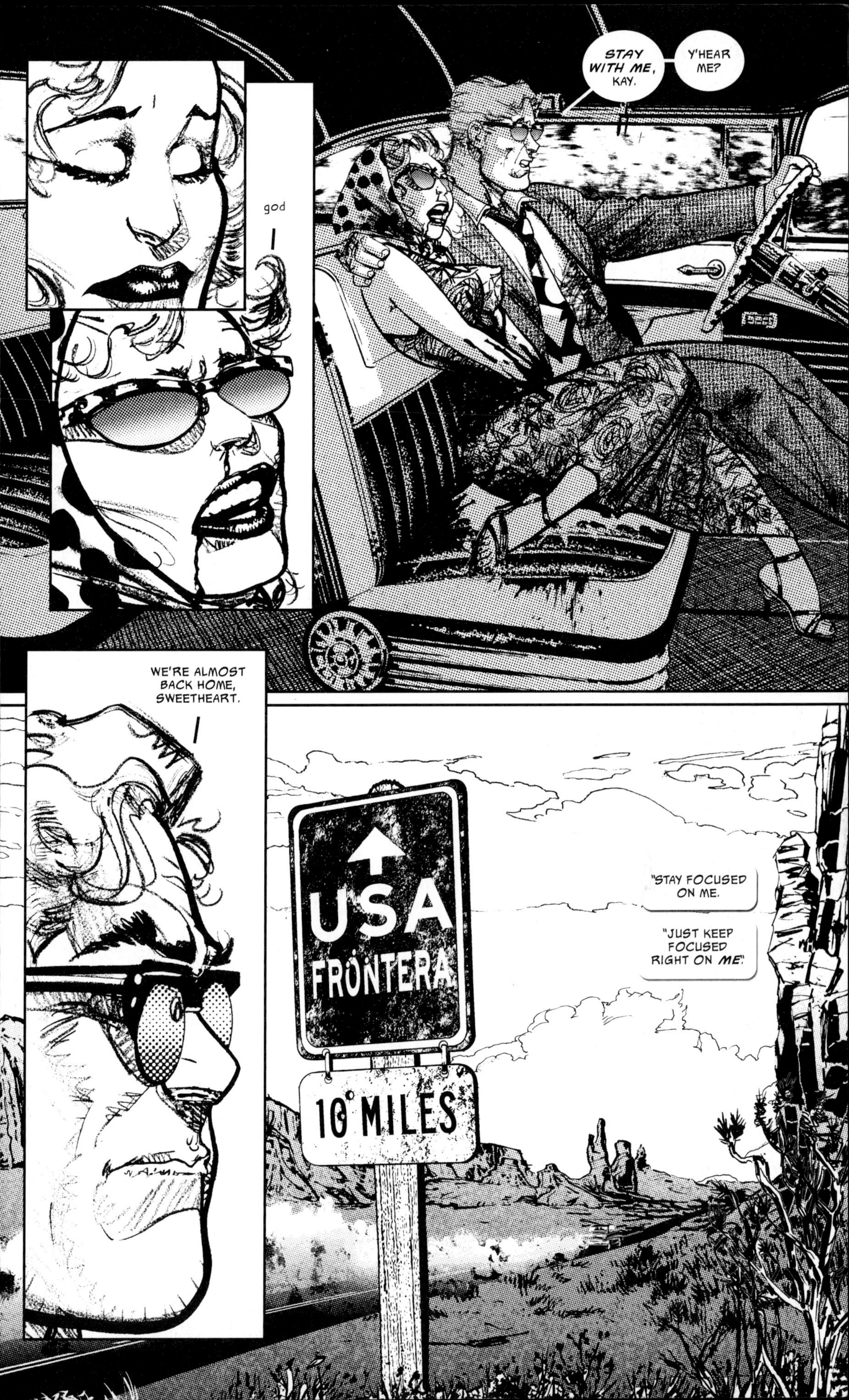
god
STAY WITH ME, KAY.
Y'HEAR ME?
WE'RE ALMOST BACK HOME, SWEETHEART.
USA
FRONTERA
10 MILES
"STAY FOCUSED ON ME.
"JUST KEEP FOCUSED RIGHT ON ME."

CAN YOU DO THAT, SWEET-HEART?
Y'KNOW, I'M DUE ONSTAGE IN AN *HOUR*...
I'LL HAVE YOU BACK BY THEN.
SORRY IT'S SO BRIGHT. THESE THINGS ARE *PIGS* FOR LIGHT. Eh, YOU'RE A SINGER, YOU'RE USED TO BRIGHT LIGHTS.
NO, NO. IT'S OKAY. IT'S *HOT* IN HERE, TOO. THIS CLOSE-- IT'S HOT.
ISN'T IT JUST.
LeMONDE
RELAX, SWEETHEART. THIS IS *TESTS*, IS ALL.
I'M TRYING TO FIGURE OUT WHAT ALL THE HELL THESE BEHEMOTHS CAN DO. THIS STUFF? TV?

NOBODY KNOWS FUCKING ANYTHING, AND I'M A GODDAMN GENIUS. SO.
SO. SEE HOW CLOSE THE CAMERA HAS TO BE TO GET YOUR FACE THAT SIZE?

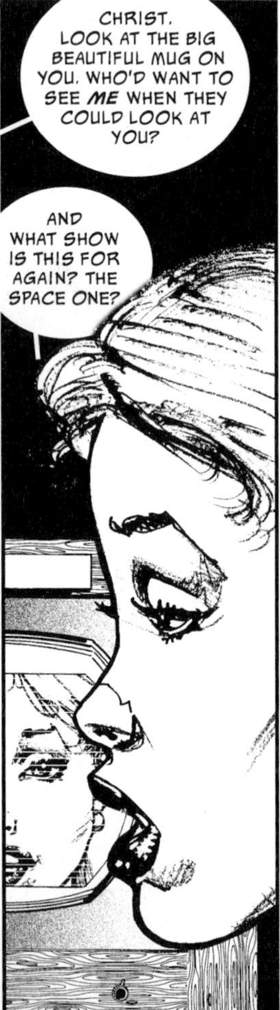
CHRIST. LOOK AT THE BIG BEAUTIFUL MUG ON YOU. WHO'D WANT TO SEE *ME* WHEN THEY COULD LOOK AT YOU?
AND WHAT SHOW IS THIS FOR AGAIN? THE SPACE ONE?

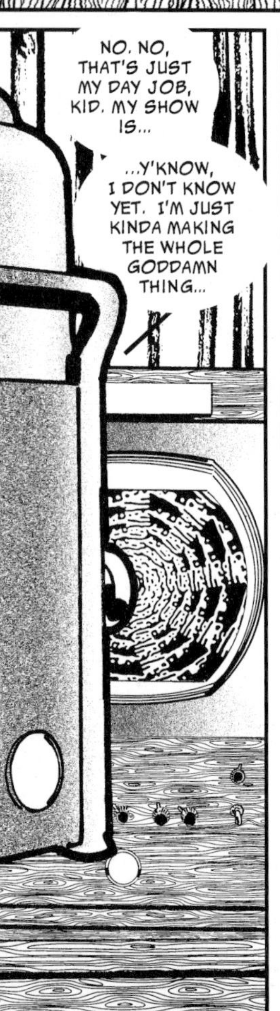
NO. NO, THAT'S JUST MY DAY JOB, KID. MY SHOW IS...
...Y'KNOW, I DON'T KNOW YET. I'M JUST KINDA MAKING THE WHOLE GODDAMN THING...

...THE FUCK IS THAT?

Huh.
NEVER THOUGHT TO POINT ONE OF THESE BIG FUCKERS AT THE MONITOR WHILE IT WAS *ON*...

GENE, EVEN IF WE CATCH ALL THE LIGHTS, IT'S FIFTEEN MINUTES--
OKAY.

GENE.
OKAY.
GENE.
YEAH. YEAH, JUST...

GENE?

Ah, GO FUCK YOURSELF, THEN.

SEE YOU 'ROUND, GENE-THE-GENIUS.
I MEAN, LOOK AT IT. IT'S JUST THE DAMNDEST THING...
CHRIST.

JUST FOUR VHF OUTLETS IN THE TOP TEN MARKETS, JUST--
--JUST GIVE ME THE FOURTH IN TEN, COMMISSIONER, I CAN--
DOCTOR--
--DOCTOR.
MR. COMMISSIONER, I'M MANUFACTURING TWENTY-INCH TELEVISIONS FOR NEXT CHRISTMAS.
TWENTY. AND IF IT WASN'T FOR MY TUBES--
--OR MY CAMERAS--
--THERE WOULDN'T BLOODY BE A TELEVISION.

THE STATIONS PICK THEIR AFFILIATIONS, DOCTOR, NOT THE FCC. AND IF THE AFFILIATES DON'T LIKE YOUR ODDS, WHAT CAN I DO?
DO WE REALLY NEED THE HAND OF GOVERNMENT MEDDLING IN THE AFFAIRS OF--

YOU CAN ARGUE ABOUT THE HAND OF THE MARKET--
--BUT YOU MEANT THE MARKET, AND YOU CAN ARGUE FOR IT ALL YOU LIKE...
I SAID "GOVERNMENT"--
...BUT, GODDAMNIT, THESE AFFILIATES HAVE OLD BUSINESS WITH THESE NETWORKS THAT DATES BACK TO RADIO.

IT'S A MONOPOLY. THE RICH GET RICHER, AND THE PEOPLE LIKE US-- THE WORKERS, THE INVENTORS, THE INNOVATORS--
--WE GET SCREWED, GODDAMNIT. I TELL YOU, IT'S UN-AMERICAN.
IT'S A CONSPIRACY!

IS IT NOW.

YES, WELL... WHY DON'T I GO ROUND UP THAT COFFEE. EXCUSE ME.
ACTUALLY...

...DO YOU MIND SHOWING ME WHERE THE LITTLE BOYS' ROOM IS AGAIN?
I COULD STAND TO FRESHEN UP.

LOVELY HOME.
Mmm.
THREE GENERATIONS NOW, MY FAMILY'S LIVED IN THIS OLD HOUSE.
SO DON'T BELIEVE MY HUSBAND'S MAN-OF-THE-PEOPLE ROUTINE.
HE MARRIED THE FIRST RICH GIRL HE COULD FIND.
THAT COFFEE POT TAKES ABOUT FIFTEEN MINUTES TO BREW.
YEAH, SO?
SO GET ON YOUR FUCKING KNEES AND GET TO WORK.

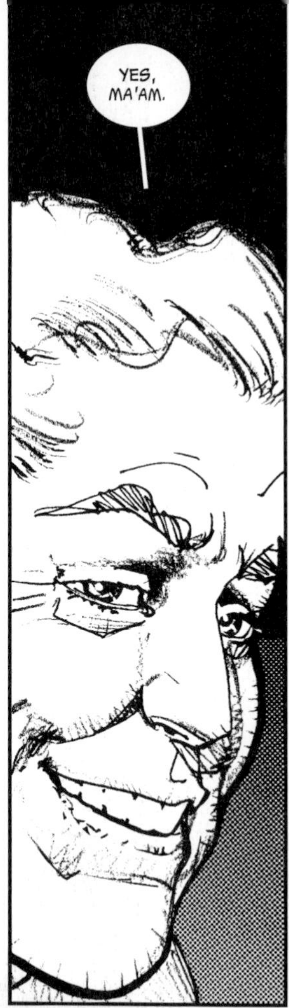
YES, MA'AM.

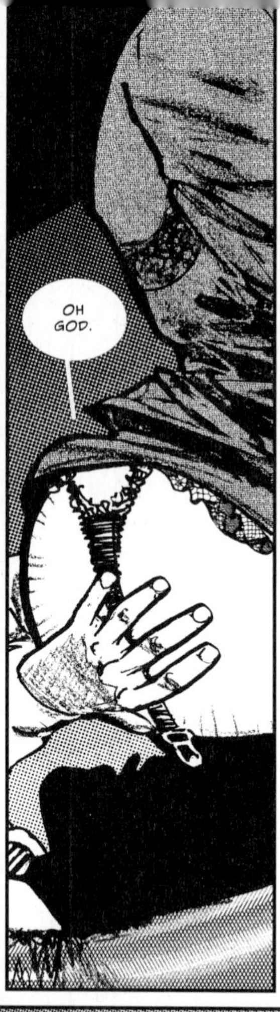
OH GOD.

C'MON. THAT'S IT.

FUCK.
FUCK, COME ON.

"COME ON.
"COME ON!"

COME ON, GODDAMNIT, SHE'S BLEEDING TO DEATH--
IN
disease

WHAT THE HELL HAPPENED?
THERE WAS... WE...
...IN MEXICO, SHE...

GOT IT.
SIR, YOU SHOULD GO WAIT OUTSIDE--
YEAH, I...
...YEAH.

SHIT.

Train to be a
NURSE
GENTLEMEN...
THIS WAY!
AND NOT IN A HOSPITAL!
THEY CARRY
disease

WHAT'S IT GONNA COST ME TO KEEP THIS OUT OF THE PAPERS?
AND DON'T BE MODEST; I'M FUCKING RICH.
AND IT WORKED. HE PAID--
--I DON'T KNOW HOW MUCH. THOUSANDS.
NO ONE EVER CAUGHT WIND OF MY TRIP SOUTH OF THE BORDER.
"I FOUND GOD THAT NIGHT. I FOUND JESUS CHRIST IN THE LIGHT OF THAT ROOM, MICHAEL.
"I MADE SO MANY PROMISES ON THAT OPERATING TABLE.
"TO CLEAN UP.
"TO FIX MY LIFE.
"TO BE A GOOD PERSON.
"YOUR FATHER SAVED MY LIFE, MICHAEL.
"AND THEN JESUS SAVED MY SOUL."
EVERYTHING ABOUT ME CHANGED ONCE I TOUCHED DEATH. I SUPPOSE VISIONS OF HEAVEN CAN DO THAT TO A PERSON.
WHAT ABOUT YOU, MICHAEL? I WORRY ABOUT YOU THESE DAYS.
EVER SINCE YOU CAME HOME YOU...
...MICHAEL, DO YOU EVER WONDER ABOUT WHAT HAPPENS TO THE SOUL AFTER DEATH?
FUCK, NO.

SO... OKAY, SO.
SO...

...AWW, C'MON...

...C'MON, C'MON--

--AWW, FUCK *ME*--

--FUCK FUCKING *FUCK*--

--OUTTA THE *WAY*--
--FUCKING TOURISTS--
--MAN'S TRYING TO GET *LAID* HERE--

IT'S NOT THE PALE MOON THAT EXCITES ME -- THAT THRILLS AND DELIGHTS ME, OH
IT'S JUST THE NEARNESS OF YOU
IT ISN'T YOUR SWEET CONVERSATION -- THAT BRINGS THIS SENSATION, OH NO
IT'S JUST THE NEARNESS OF YOU
WHEN I FEEL YOU IN MY ARMS AND I FEEL YOU SO CLOSE TO ME
ALL MY WILDEST DREAMS COME TRUE
I NEED NO SOFT LIGHTS TO ENCHANT ME IF YOU'LL ONLY GRANT ME THE RIGHT
TO HOLD YOU EVER SO TIGHT
AW, EVIE, NO.
'SCUSE ME, SIR; THE LADY'S ASKED IF YOU'D REMOVE YOURSELF FROM THE CLUB.
AND TO FEEL IN THE NIGHT
YOU GOTTA BE FUCKING *KIDDING* ME, PAL.
LADY SCRATCHED HER FACE. COULDA BEEN SCRATCHING IT AT ANY ONE OF THESE ASSHOLES YOU GOT IN HERE TONIGHT.
WHO THE FUCK DO YOU--
THE NEARNESS OF YOU

Leon & Eddie's 4 COMPLETE SETS NIGHTLY BAR
MOTHER-FUCKER--
--FUCKIN' THINK YOU CAN--
--FU-UHHF!
EASY THERE, SIR--
WHHFF
--HAVE A NICE NIGHT NOW.
Ah, GOD-DAMNIT.

HOWDY, FOLKS.
SORRY TO KEEP YOU WAITING.
WELL THEN NOW.
WHAT DID I MISS?
...DID YOU MAKE THE COFFEE?

SORRY FOR, Uh...FOR THE STATE OF THE PLACE.
GET YOU A DRINK?
I DON'T DRINK. NO THANK YOU.
AND IT'S ALL RIGHT. YOU'VE HAD SO MUCH ON YOUR...
...MIND.

SURE.
SOME-THING LIKE THAT.
THIS WASN'T--
--Ahh--
--YOUR FATHER NEVER BROUGHT ME HERE. WE HAD...
...WELL, WE WENT OTHER PLACES.
THIS LOOKS ABOUT RIGHT, THOUGH.
WHAT DO YOU MEAN?
HE...
...YOUR FATHER KNEW WHAT HE WANTED, MICHAEL. HE HAD--

--HE HAD HIS WAYS, MICHAEL. HOW EXPLICIT MUST I GET?
I WAS IN MY CUPS AND YOUR FATHER SUGGESTED WE GET SOME AIR...
...THEN THE NEXT THING YOU'D KNOW, WE WERE IN A ROOM SOMEWHERE AND HE..

...WANTED T'FUCK ME? WELL, C'MON THEN, WHIP THAT SHHHIT OUT, BIG MAN.
SHIT. I DON'T GIVE A FUCK. LESH FUCK, C'MON.

HANG ON.
I WANT TO REMEMBER YOU JUST LIKE THIS.

...PULLED OUT HIS CAMERA. HE STARTED DIRECTING ME.
HE ONLY DID IT THAT FIRST TIME, AND NEVER AGAIN.
I WAS WITH HIM OTHER TIMES--WITH--OTHER GIRLS SOMETIMES, BUT HE'D ONLY SHOOT THEM, AND...
...AND I PRETENDED I DIDN'T REMEMBER, BUT I DID.
I REMEMBER, EVERYTHING.

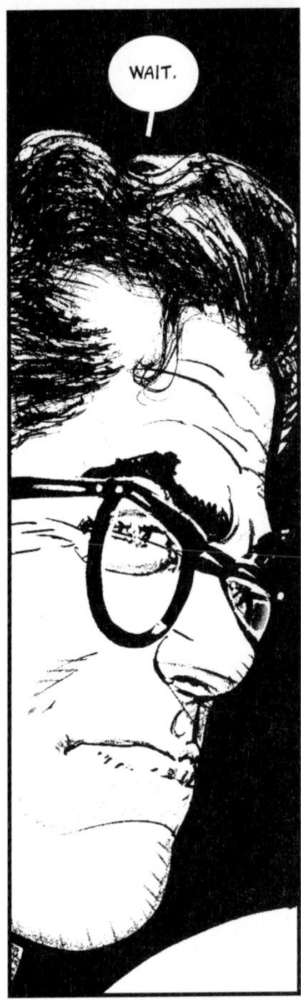
WAIT.

MICHAEL, DON'T POINT THAT CAMERA AT--
POP!

POP!
MAYBE ONE WITHOUT THE BOTTLE.

YOU'RE NOT GONNA DO ANYTHING WITH THOSH PICTURESH AREYA?
GOTTA CAREER TA CONSHIDDER.
NAH. THESE'RE JUST FOR ME.
I WANT TO REMEMBER YOU LIKE THIS. TONIGHT, THIS TIME, THIS PLACE, YOU, ME...
...THAT INCREDIBLE ASS OF YOURS...
ALL THIS SHIT, LITTLE GIRL. ONE DAY ALL OF IT'LL GO AWAY.
ONE DAY EVERY-BODY'LL BE ALONE.

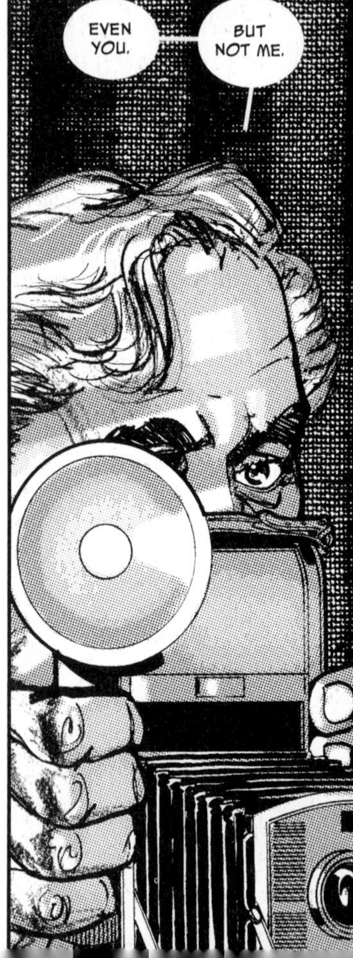
EVEN YOU.
BUT NOT ME.

pop!

WHAT THE HELL IS THE MATTER WITH YOU--
KARA, WAIT--

--TAKE MY PICTURE IN A PLACE LIKE THIS--
KARA.

WHAT, YOU--
--YOU ASSHOLE, YOU--
THE CAMERAS ALL HAD FILM IN THEM.
I DON'T...
ALL OF THE CAMERAS HAD FRESH FILM IN THEM. READY TO GO. NOT A FRAME SHOT.
COPS FIGURED HE'D HIRED SOME PRO-SKIRT AND HE HAD A HEART ATTACK IN THE MIDDLE OF IT ALL, SO SHE SPLIT, AND...
...YOU SAID HE TOOK PICTURES THE FIRST TIME HE WAS WITH HIS GIRLS, AND JUST THE FIRST TIME, RIGHT?
NO PHOTOS WERE TAKEN WHEN HE DIED. I CHECKED THE CAMERAS.

I THINK THAT WOMAN'S PHOTOGRAPH IS SOMEWHERE IN THIS ROOM.
THE GIRL HE WAS WITH WHEN HE DIED IS HERE SOMEWHERE.
YOU SURE YOU DON'T WANT A DRINK ?

...IT'S JUST DA NEARNESS... OF YOUZZE...
CARLYLE WHITE
Uh, MR. WHITE AROUND? CARLYLE WHITE?
NO. WHAT?
NO. SORRY. HE, Uh--HE'S GONE.
HE DIED.
Ah. SORRY. TA HEAR IT.
STILL, I GOT LAST WEEK'S KINESCOPES FROM THE LAB, WHERE YA WANT 'EM?
CARLYLE WHITE
NO, I DON'T--
--THOSE DON'T BELONG HERE. THEY GET SHIPPED TO L.A. FOR NEXT WEEK'S REBROADCAST.
NO, DAT'S A SEPARATE T'ING. I DID DAT DIS MORNING.
THIS IS MR. WHITE'S BATCH. BEEN LIKE DIS EVERY WEEK FOR YEARS.
EVERY WEEK?
LIKE CLOCKWORK, HONEY.
WHERE DID HE PUT THEM ALL..?

SATELLITE SAM

4: COOKIEPUSHER

MOMMA! COME IN, COME IN. MARIA! SHE'S HERE!

MARIA!
OH MY GOODNESS.
COMING, I'M COMING--
MARIA!
HERE, MOMMA, LET ME TAKE YOUR COAT--
REALLY, JOSEPH, I'M CAPABLE OF TAKING OFF MY--

MARIA, MOMMA, MOMMA--
MARI-ANGELA MELATO, MOMMA. IS SO NICE--
IT'S.

IT'S NICE TO MEET YOU. FINALLY.
SEEMS LIKE IT'S BEEN YEARS SINCE MY JOSEPH STARTED TALKING ABOUT YOU.
IT HAS BEEN TOO LONG, MOMMA. YES.
COFFEE? I'M JUST FINISHING UP THE SALAD.

zbbbvba
GREASY WOP FINGERS TOUCHING MY FOOD
azzrburubb

...THE CROWD HERE, EAGERLY AWAITING THE APPEARANCE OF MR. KARNES ON WHAT PROMISES TO BE AN EXCITING DAY IN NEW YORK POLITICS-
OKAY, BACK TO ONE.
THE FUCK ANNOUNCES THEY'RE RUNNING FOR OFFICE THIRTEEN MONTHS OUT DURING A PENNANT RACE?
Karnes ★ for ★ Congress
LEMONDE

GENE.
JACKIE, GET IN THERE ON HIM-GIVE ME A COWBOY WITH SOME OF THE PODIUM AND STAY THERE, PLEASE.
WHAT? I'M SERIOUS, IKE.
ANYBODY THAT'S GONNA VOTE FOR THIS CLOWN'S EITHER *LISTENING* TO THE GAME OR *AT IT.*
I SHOULD BE LISTENING TO IT.
ALSO, THE DISH IS GOOFY.

WHAT DOES THAT MEAN, EXACTLY?
UPLINK'S GOOD *ENOUGH*, BUT SOMEBODY'S GOTTA FIX THE DISH LATER.
BUT NOW? AND DO YOU HAVE *MONEY* ON THIS GAME, BY CHANCE?
IT'S GOOD ENOUGH. AND YES. GO DODGERS.
THE FUCK ARE WE DOING OUT *HERE* INSTEAD OF PUTTING ON THE HIGHEST-RATED SHOW ON THIS *FARKAKTE* NETWORK?
I SWEAR TO MY SWEET AUNT SALLY, IT'S LIKE THIS WHOLE WORLD'S GONE NUCKING *FUTS*.
DON'T YOU KNOW WHO REB KARNES IS, GENE?
HERE HE COMES. LOOK LIVELY ...NOW.
AND HERE HE IS, THE MAN OF THE MOMENT...WILSON "REB" KARNES AND HIS LOVELY WIFE JEANIE, TAKING THE STAGE TO A WARM ROUND OF APPLAUSE...

THANK YOU, LADIES AND GENTLEMEN, FOR THAT WARM WELCOME.
THE LATE CONGRESSMAN MURRAY IS IRREPLACEABLE. I THINK WE ALL KNOW THAT. I'M NOT HERE TO REPLACE HIM.
Karnes for Congress
TWO, JACKIE.
KARNES IS GINSBERG'S MAN ON THE FCC.
S'WHY WE'RE HERE, GENE.
"YOU ASK DOC, KARNES IS SUPPOSED TO OPEN UP THE AIRWAVES TO LeMONDE AND SAVE ALL OUR SORRY SOULS.
"SO THE GOOD DOCTOR PRE-EMPTS SATELLITE SAM TO AIR HIS LAUNCH PARTY. CALL IT A CAMPAIGN CONTRIBUTION.
"BACK TO ONE."
BUT WE CAN ALL KEEP FIGHTING THE WAY HE DID...
...FOR THE GOOD PEOPLE OF THE GREAT STATE OF NEW YORK...
...AND OUR CHILDREN, AND OUR FAMILIES!
GIANTS WIN AND I'LL FIX THE DISH BACK AT THE SHOP. MY DODGERS DO IT AND IT'S YOU.
YOU'RE ON, SHMUCK.
PUT KARNES IN CONGRESS AND KEEP WASHINGTON RED FREE...

"...AND PINK FREE! LET'S KEEP AMERICA FOR AMERICANS!"
SWEET-HEART, THEY FIRED ME.
CARLO...?
...WHAT'S GOING ON?
MISSED YOU AT CRAIG'S THE OTHER NIGHT. EVERYONE WAS THERE.
BRUCE SAID YOU'D RSVP'D, SO WHEN YOU DIDN'T ARRIVE WE ALL WORRIED YOU HAD A STROKE...

WHAT? WHY?

YOU REMEMBER THAT LITTLE COOKIE-PUSHER BOY I HAD IN THE PAGE PROGRAM, WITH THE CHEEKBONES AND THOSE HOT LITTLE BLOWJOB LIPS?
OF COURSE. I'M NOT DEAD.

WELL, SHE AND I, WE WENT FOR A WALK TO CRAIG'S. MET FOR A FEW DRINKS, THEN WE'D STROLL UP THE PARK TO THE WEST SIDE.
SEE WHERE THE NIGHT TOOK US.

WELL IT TOOK US INTO THE PARK. LOTS OF QUEENS WERE OUT...

...AND IT WASN'T SO COLD THAT STOPPING SEEMED LIKE A HALF-BAD PROPOSITION.

ANNNND? HOW WAS HE?
FUCKING SINISTER, DARLING.

IN ALL THE KERFUFFLE, THE FUCKING COCKCHAFER KEPT MY *UNDERPANTS.*
MONDAY MORNING, HE WALKED RIGHT INTO GINSBERG'S OFFICE, DROPPED THEM ON HIS DESK, AND INSISTED I'D TRIED TO RAPE HIM IN THE LOCKERS.
THEN HE DEMANDED A RAISE AND A PROMOTION.
OH MY *LORD.*

GINSBERG FIRED ME. RIGHT THERE ON THE SPOT. I NEVER WAS THE *BUTCHEST* IN THE WORLD, BUT I THOUGHT I WAS AT LEAST PASSING.
...AW, CARLO...

AT LEAST THEY FIRED HER, TOO. BLACKMAILERS AND HOMOS: NEITHER SHALL WE HERE AT LeMONDE ABIDE.
I WAS FIRED FOR BEING THE REALLY WRONG KIND OF PINK. "*THERE WILL BE NO LIABILITIES AT THE LeMONDE NETWORK,*" HE TOLD ME.
CARLO...

..THE *HELL?*

HAM, I SAID.
GOOD LUCK, PAL. DON'T LET THE BASTARDS GET YOU DOWN.
Hmm.
JESUS, YOU'RE NOT EVEN LISTENING TO ME.
I'M SAYING ALL WE DO TOMORROW IS CARRY THE DUMMY STICK IN ONE SCENE AND ASK QUESTIONS IN ANOTHER.
WHAT?

NO--
NO NO *NO*--
GOD *DAMNIT*, I TOLD HIM, THAT LITTLE QUEER--
I KNOW, RIGHT?
--I TOLD THAT LITTLE QUEER I WILL BE DEAD AND BURIED BEFORE HE DOESN'T TAKE MY GODDAMN NOTES.
HIYAH, *BOSS*! WHAT'S THE *GOOD* NEWS?
THE FUCK'S THE *MATTER* WITH YOU TWO? YOU HAVE THE DAY OFF.
FUCKING *ACTORS*.
CHRIST.

LIBBY? WHERE THE FUCK ARE YOU? ARE YOU HERE?
I CALLED A MEETING AT FOUR, LIBBY, AND GODDAMNIT, IT'S FOUR...
SHH.
BOBBY THOMSON... UP THERE SWINGIN'...
...HE'S HAD TWO OUT OF THREE, A SINGLE AND A DOUBLE...
...AND BILLY COX IS PLAYING HIM RIGHT ON THE THIRD BASE LINE...
ONE OUT, LAST OF THE NINTH...

IT'S 3:57 AND WE'RE NOT EVEN ON THE AIR TODAY, AND SHH.
BRANCA PITCHES...
YES. AND WE NOW HAVE TO FIGURE OUT HOW TO GET OUR THREE REMAINING DAYS OF BULLSHIT DOWN TO TWO. TURN IT OFF.
...BOBBY THOMSON TAKES A STRIKE CALLED ON THE INSIDE CORNER...

BOBBY HITTING AT .292...
FNAK
GOD-DAMNIT...
WHAT THE FUCK IS ALL THIS SHIT? YOU STARTING A NICKELODEON?
(sigh)
KINE-SCOPES.
SO YOU SEND 'EM TO THE WAREHOUSE ON 66th. WHY THE FUCK ARE THEY IN YOUR--
CARLYLE'S OFFICE. AND THEY'RE HIS KINNIES.
IT'S A DIFFERENT THING.
HE WAS PAYING FOR IT OUT OF HIS OWN POCKET--
--AND MUST'VE BEEN TAKING 'EM HOME HIMSELF.
JESUS, WAS THERE EVER A MAN MORE OBSESSED WITH PRESERVING HIS OWN IMAGE?
WHAT?

NOTHING. IT'S JUST A WHOLE LOT OF TROUBLE AND MONEY FOR THIS BULLSHIT.
HE JUST, WHAT, HE HAS KINNIES OF EVERY-THING?
NEAR AS I CAN FIGURE. OF SATELLITE SAM, ANYWAY.
WHAT DO WE DO WITH THE KINESCOPES, ANYWAY? JUST STORE 'EM FOREVER?
NOTHING. THEY'RE SHITTY. THEY REBROADCAST FOR SHIT. DOC INSISTS ON SHOOTING THEM IN 16--SO WE SHOOT SHIT IN 16 MILLIMETERS.
WAREHOUSE CATALOGS 'EM AND SHIPS 'EM WEST TO THE AFFILIATES NOT ON OUR PIPE. CHICAGO, DETROIT, KANSAS CITY, ASS-END, FUCKSBURGH, WHER-EVER CANNIBALISM IS STILL PRACTICED.

REALLY, WE ONLY PULL 'EM OUT TO RE-RUN IN THE OFF-WEEKS, IF THERE'S NOT SPECIAL PROGRAMMING.
THAT'S IT? NO WONDER NOBODY COULD TELL ME ON THE PHONE.

WELL, IN THEORY, WHEN THE FCC LETS US GO COAST-TO-COAST WE'LL MAKE COPIES FOR EVERY AFFILIATE.
WE SHOOT HERE, SHIP FROM HERE, AND THREE DAYS LATER THEY'RE REBROAD-CASTING.
IF THE NETWORK WAS ALREADY DOING IT, WHY WOULD CARLYLE DO IT, TOO?
THE FUCK SHOULD I KNOW? THE OLD MAN WAS WEIRD. HE WAS A COLLECTOR. WHO KNOWS?
SO WHAT HAPPENS WHEN CALIFORNIA'S DONE WITH 'EM?

THEY SEND 'EM BACK HERE, WE PUT 'EM IN THE WARE-HOUSE ON 66, THEN ONCE A YEAR MEN IN TRUCKS COME, LOAD 'EM ALL UP, AND DUMP 'EM IN THE EAST FUCKING RIVER.
MEETING. NOW, PLEASE. AND DON'T WORRY ABOUT YOUR BALL GAME. THE DODGERS ARE UNSTOPPABLE.

"...AND PLEASE FIND MY WRITER AND BRING HIM WITH YOU."
ISN'T THERE--
ISN'T THERE--
HAMILTON.
WARDROBE
HAM.
IT'S A FIFTEEN MINUTE SHOW. THERE'S ONLY--
--IT'S A FIFTEEN MINUTE SHOW OF WHICH YOU ARE NOT THE STAR, AND--
--HAM, CLINT, LOOK, I KNOW MIKE'S NOT HIS FATHER IN FRONT OF THE CAMERA, BUT...
BUT WHAT, GUY, BUDDY, PAL. COME ON--
--WE'RE JUST SAYIN', LET MIKEY FIND HIS SEA LEGS A LITTLE WHILE, YEAH?
LET HIM GET USED TO IT. FOR CHRIST'S SAKE.
YOU'RE PUTTIN' HIM FRONT AND CENTER ALL THE TIME.
MICHAEL, BLESS HIM, IS NEITHER A THESPIAN-BORN NOR TRAINED, GUY.
AND THE PROGRAM--
--YOUR WORDS, GUY--
--SUFFERS. HE LOSES TRACK.
STOPS PAYING ATTENTION TO THE SCENE, AND--
GUY?
GUY.
GUY. DICK'S THING.
RIGHT. YES. OKAY.
HAM, I'LL TAKE ANOTHER PASS.
YEAH.

WE NEED TO CRUSH THE LAST THREE DAYS OF THE WEEK INTO TWO-
YEAH. I ALREADY--
--THE STAR PIRATES HAVE SOME KIND OF ATOMIC-ASSHOLE-VOODOO-BULLSHIT THING. I CAN GET US THERE.
WOW. YOU JUST HAVE A FIX LIKE THAT READY TO GO? WASN'T THAT --GUY, THIS WAS YOUR STORY.
Mm.
FUCK THIS JOB.
AAAYYY!!!
THE GIANTS WON THE FUCKIN' PENNANT!
ARE YOU KIDDIN' ME?!?
WAIT, WHAT?
THE...
...MY DODGERS LOST?
...
FUCK THIS JOB.

1948
1949
1950
1951

IT'S IN THIS ROOM.
EVERY-THING IS IN THIS GODDAMN ROOM.

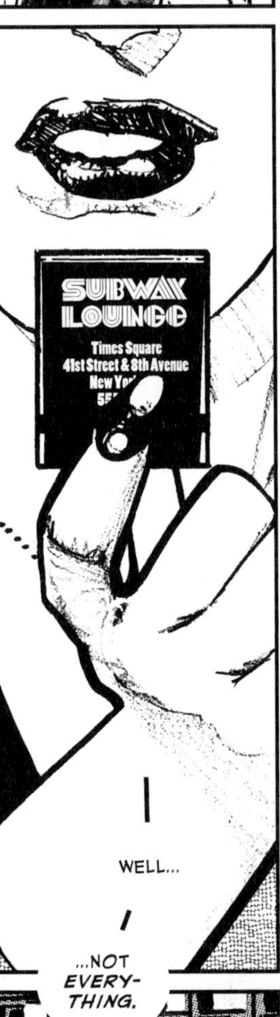
SUBWAY LOUNGE
Times Square
41st Street & 8th Avenue
WELL...
...NOT EVERY-THING.

SWING CLUB
SUBWAY LOUNGE

MY OLD FLAME

BUT IT'S

MY OLD FLAME,

MY NEW LOVERS ALL

SEEM SO TAME.

BOURBON, NEAT.
THANKS.

SMOOTH.
HA *HA.*
HEY.
WE GONNA HAVE A BEEF, PAL?
WHAT? NO-- NOTHING LIKE THAT. I THOUGHT...
...THOUGHT SHE WAS SOMEONE ELSE. LEMME GET TWO SODA WATERS?
ONE. I'M FINE, MIKE...
SOME *TEE-TOTALER.*
LOOK, IF YOUR *GIRLFRIEND* HERE CHANGES HER MIND AND WANTS A REAL DRINK, LADY, YOU JES' LET ME KNOW.
WILL DO.
THAT LOOKS LIKE THE GIRL FROM--
--THE HEELS, ON THE *SINK*--
YEAH, MAYBE. COULD BE--
--ONLY ONE WAY TO *FIND OUT*...

N & EDDIE
Air Cooled
Leon & Ec
NOT TONIGHT, PAL.

OH FOR THE LOVE OF FUCKING *FUCK*--
SAID NOT *TONIGHT.*
--I'LL BE GOOD! I'LL BE *QUIET*--

--YOU'LL BE LOOKING FOR YOUR FUCKING *TEETH* TWO BLOCKS UP ON *QUEER STREET.*

HEY HEY *HEY*, WATCH THE *HAVANA*.
NOT.
TONIGHT.

CHRIST. ALL RIGHT, ALL *RIGHT*...

IF IT'S 3:45 AND YOU'VE DIALED UP LEMONDE, THEN IT MUST BE TIME FOR...
LEMONDE

...SATELLIIIIIIIIITE SAMMMMMMM!"
SATELLITE SAM

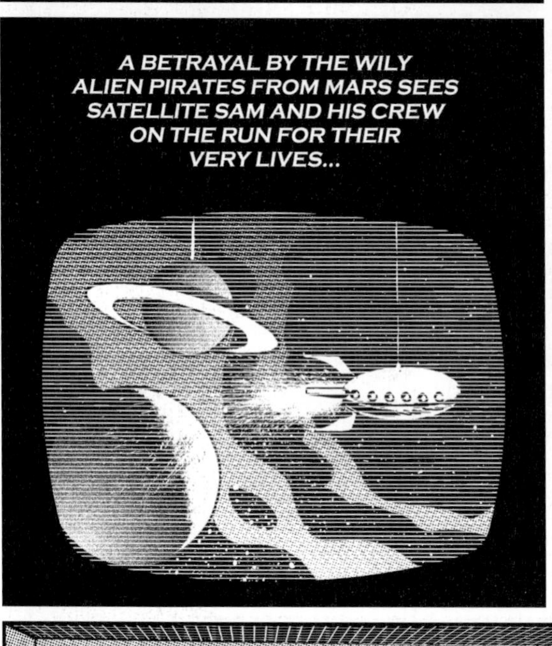
A BETRAYAL BY THE WILY ALIEN PIRATES FROM MARS SEES SATELLITE SAM AND HIS CREW ON THE RUN FOR THEIR VERY LIVES...

MAJOR MELINDA! DAMAGE REPORT!
IT'S BAD, SAM. THE MARTIAN STAR PIRATES REALLY RANG OUR BELL!
YOU'VE GOT TO GET ME THE POWER I NEED TO GET US TO SAFETY!

AND GO THREE.
GO THREE.
fiing.

MY, SAM, WHAT ON EARTH COULD HAVE CAUSED SUCH DAMAGE?
I DON'T KNOW, COLONEL TRUE. SOME KIND OF... EXPERIMENTAL WEAPON, I IMAGINE.

THEY MUST HAVE... AN ATOMIC ACCELERATOR!
A WHO-MIC WHAT-CELE-WHAT?

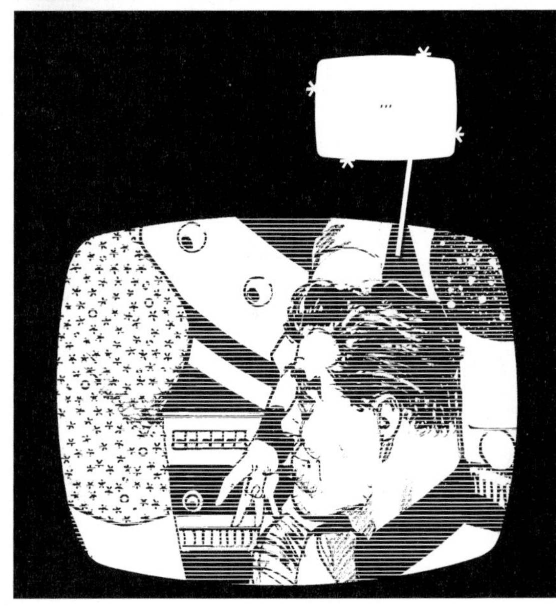
...

erm-- "ATOMIC ACCELERATOR," CLINT, OLD CHUM!
A GRAND WEAPON THAT SPEWS FORTH NUCLEAR FIRE.

OH, GOD DAMNIT!
BACK TO ONE, MIKE'S CHECKED OUT--
--CHECKING OUT HER ASS LIKE EVERY OTHER BOY IN AMERICA--
--SHUT THE FUCK UP, JACKIE, OR I'LL BUST YOU BACK DOWN TO ELECTRIC--
--THREE, GET ON HAM AND STAY THERE IN CASE MIKEY DROPS ANOTHER GODDAMN LINE--
chht!
HE'S PLOWED. ONE'S UP-

...AND IF WE CAN'T GET THE SHIP REPAIRED WHILE OUTRACING THESE...BLOODY MARTIANS...
...EARTH SHALL BE NEXT! Erm--
--ISN'T THAT RIGHT, SATELLITE SAM?

WELL, FOR OUR SAKE AND YOURS, UH, SAM, WE HOPE YOUR MISSION IS A SUCCESS! BUT TO FIND OUT FOR SURE, WE'LL HAVE TO TUNE IN TOMORROW, FOR ANOTHER EPISODE OF... SATELLIIIIIIIIITE SAMMMMMMM!
SATELLITE SAM

GOD FUCKING DAMNIT--!
GOOD ENOUGH SHOW, EVERY-BODY.
COULD SOMEONE RING THE GOOD DOCTOR?

MICHAEL WHITE
"SATELLITE SAM"
MICHAEL WHITE
"SATELLITE SAM"
"I'D LIKE HIM TO CHECK IN ON HIS STAR PATIENT..."
SON OF A BITCH--
MICHAEL.
DO YOU FEEL BETTER NOW, AT LEAST?
DOC...
...I'M SORRY, DOC. I TRY AND I TRY AND--
--AND I'M JUST NOT GETTING IT. FUCKING FIRE ME, CANCEL THE SHOW, JUST GET IT OVER WITH AND STOP MAKING ME MAKE AN ASS OUT OF MYSELF FIVE TIMES A WEEK ON TELEVISION.
YOU CAN PLEASE DEDUCT WHAT FIXING THE ROOM COSTS FROM MY PAY.
OH, DON'T WORRY-- I WILL.
AND DON'T WORRY ABOUT YOU, EITHER, MICHAEL. IF IT WAS EASY, EVERYONE WOULD BE A TV STAR.
YOUR CONTRACT, AND THE LICENSE LeMONDE HAS ON SATELLITE SAM IS UP VERY SOON--SO MAYBE THIS WILL SET YOUR MIND AT EASE.
YOUR FATHER LOVED THIS SHOW, HE LOVED THE LeMONDE NETWORK, AND HE LOVED NEW YORK CITY.
AND WE FEEL THE SAME ABOUT HIM, YOU AND THE SHOW.
I HAD PAPERS DRAWN UP REFLECTING AS MUCH.
FUCK LeMONDE AND GINSBERG AND HIS VIDEO CAMERAS.

YOU DID WHAT?
IT'S AN OFFER, MICHAEL. YOUR FATHER AND I HAD AGREED ON CERTAIN NUMBERS AND TERMS, AND THAT'S A WRITTEN RECORD OF THOSE TERMS.
I WANT YOU, AND SATELLITE SAM, TO STAY PUT.
TO STAY HOME.
AND I'LL MAKE YOU A VERY WEALTHY MAN IN THE PROCESS.
NEED A DRINK TO CELEBRATE? I'VE BROUGHT JUST THE THING.
I...
OKAY. I...
NO, DOC. NO...
...IT'S...
NO THANK YOU.
THANK YOU FOR THE OFFER, THE OFFERS, BUT I--
--I'M PRETTY SURE A DRINK IS THE LAST THING I NEED.

SATELLITE SAM

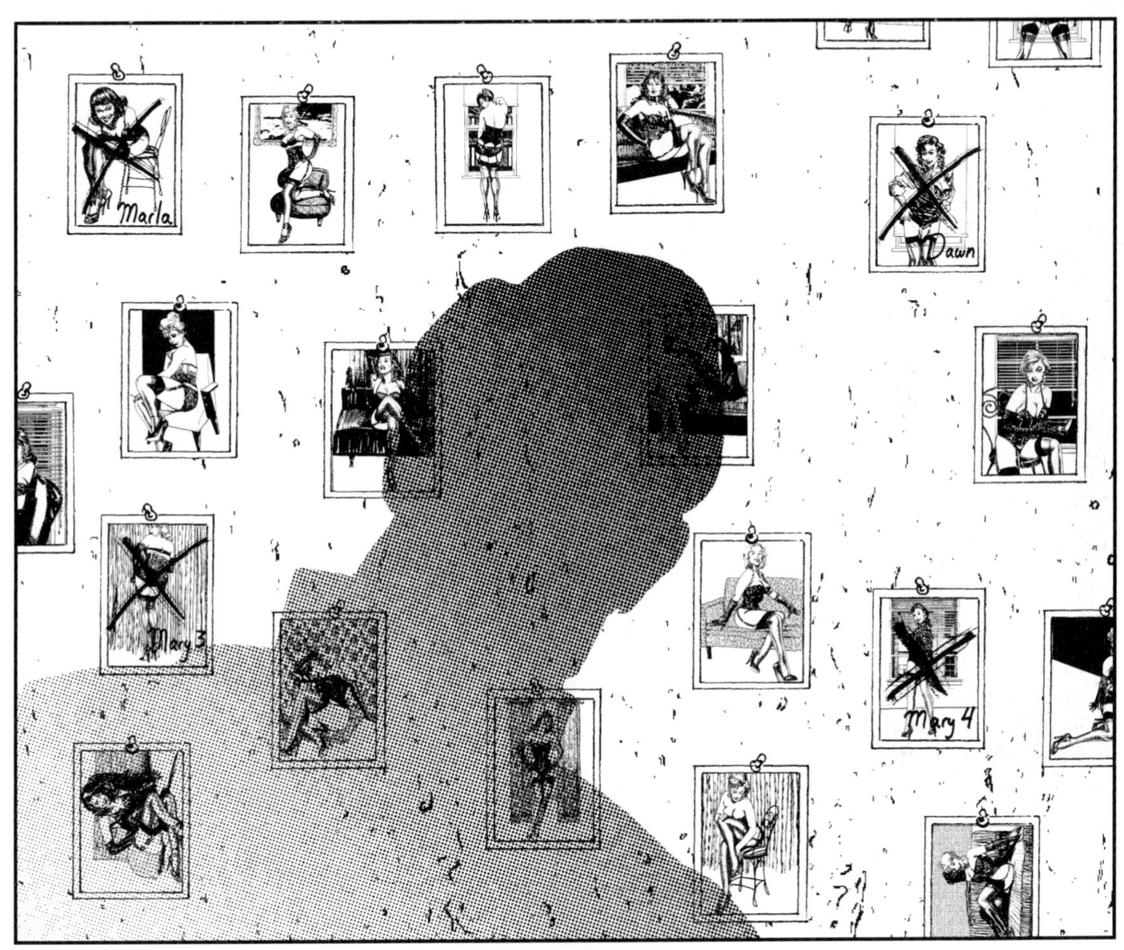

5: JOBS

MARLA. —— MARY 3. —— DAWN. —— MARY 4. ——

WHO WAS CARLYLE WHITE?
AND WHY THESE WOMEN? WHY DID HE KEEP THIS LITTLE PIECE OF THEM?
EVERY GIRL WE FIND, OR EVERY FRIEND OF HERS, OR FRIEND OF A FRIEND... NOBODY KNOWS.
THEY'RE JUST A BUNCH OF CHEAP OLD WHORES WITH NOTHING TO SAY...
MICHAEL.

FEEL THIS.
I DON'T...
MOST OF THE... "LINGERIE" HERE...THAT YOUR FATHER ACQUIRED...
IT'S...CHEAP. IT'S -- WELL, IT WOULD BE FINANCIALLY APPROPRIATE TO MOST OF THE WOMEN TO WHOM WE'VE SPOKEN.
BUT THIS ONE... FEEL IT.
FRENCH SILK. AND THERE'S A PERFUME ON IT I CAN'T PLACE, BUT I KNOW I'VE SMELLED IT BEFORE.
A WEALTHY WOMAN WORE THIS.
...MICHAEL?
GINSBERG OFFERED TO MAKE ME RICH.
...
...DID YOU TELL HIM YES ?
I DIDN'T TELL HIM ANYTHING.
C'MON...

"...IT'S THE WITCHING HOUR."
...TIME IS UPON US NOW, FRIENDS. IN MANHATTAN, IN QUEENS--
--IN BROOKLYN AND LONG ISLAND AND THE BRONX--
--ALL GOOD MEN MUST STAND UP AND SAY, WE DID NOT FIGHT--
--AT GUADALCANAL AND NORMANDY, AT ANZIO AND THE BULGE--

-OVER MIDWAY AND HERE AT HOME, TO LET--
--SUBVERSIVE FOREIGN INFLUENCES SEEP INTO OUR NATIONAL CHARACTER!

A VOTE FOR KARNES IS MORE THAN A VO FOR NEV YORK--
HOW COULD HE OFFER THAT?
I THOUGHT LeMONDE WAS WAITING FOR THE FCC.
I THOUGHT WE NEED MORE AFFILATES.
IT'S A VOTE FOR AMERICA!

FOR THE AMERICAN WAY OF LIFE!
BECAUSE I'M A NEW YORKER, BORN AND RAISED, FOLKS--
...

--I'M NOT FROM ITHACA OR ALBANY, OR EVEN--
--MASSA-CHUSETTS, LIKE MY OPPONENT--
HERE, CABBIE.

--NEW YORK CITY IS WHERE I MADE MY HOME. I KNOW THE CITY AND HER STREETS--
BAR

--AND IT'S NEW YORK CITY THAT'S GOING TO COME WITH ME ALL THE WAY TO WASHINGTON --
--AND MAKE THIS NATION A STRONGER, BETTER PLACE!
AAAAAAUUUGGHH
FUCK, MADDIE, FUCK--
--FUCK, I SOUNDED GOOD OUT THERE TODAY--

FUUAAHH GOD, NOT SO FAST NOT SO FAST!
MMM MMM?

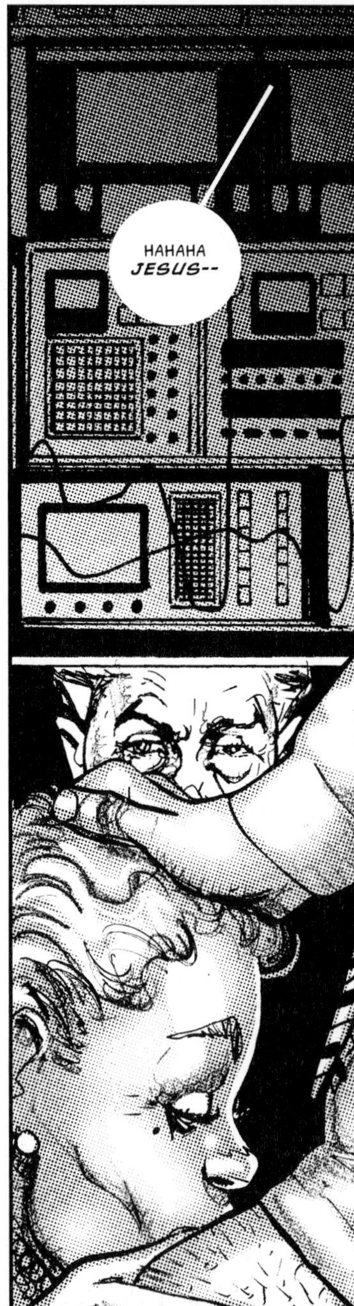
HAHAHA JESUS--

Nnf.
Nnf.
HELLO?

DOC?
TH' HELL?
AH! EUGENE, EUGENE.
GOOD EVENING.
LeMONDE

WHAT'CHA *DOIN'* THERE, DOC?
JUST ADMIRING THE... CRAFTSMANSHIP OF THE *LeMONDE MOBILECASTER ONE* HERE.
HELL OF A THING, ISN'T SHE?
JUST A HELL OF A THING.

SURE, DOC, IF YOU SAY SO...
SAY, GENE, I'VE NOT EVER HAD TO *RUN* A BROADCAST FROM IN THERE-- IS THERE TOO MUCH LIGHT FROM THE WINDOWS? CAN YOU WORK OKAY INSIDE?
DOC, IT'S DARK AND HOT AND FUCKING AWFUL IN THERE.
IT'S A THREE-MAN DONKEY SHOW IN A ONE-MAN SUBMARINE, WRAPPED WITH CHRISTMAS LIGHTS.
WE CLIMB UP ON THE ROOF WHEN WE CAN--
--RATHER DIRECT HALF-BLIND OVER DYING OF *HEAT EXHAUSTION*, TELL YOU THE TRUTH.
ALSO, THE DISH IS WITCHY AND I LOST A *BET*, SO I GOTTA FIX IT.
NOT NECESSARY.

ON THE CONTRARY, THE DISH IS PRETTY FUCKING IMPORTANT TO THE OPERATION--
TONIGHT, I'M SAYING, GENE. IT'S NEAR TEN O'CLOCK AND YOU'VE GOT *SHOWS* TOMORROW...

...AND BESIDES--
--I'D MUCH RATHER YOU TELL ME MORE ABOUT THIS IDEA OF YOURS.
REALLY?
YES.
AS A PIONEER, AND DARE I SAY IT, VISIONARY IN THIS NEWBORN BUSINESS OF OURS, I'M ALWAYS ON THE LOOKOUT FOR OTHERS WITH INTERESTING THINGS TO SAY.
SO I'M SAYING, SAY IT.
WELL, DOC, I LIKE TO MAKE PEOPLE LAUGH. INCORRIGIBLE SMARTASS. ALWAYS WAS. AND IT SEEMS TO ME--
--TV, SEE, IT'S--IT'S WORDS AND PICTURES. AND WE FORGET THAT SO FAR. BUT WE TELL STORIES TOO MUCH BY SHOWING AND TELLING.
BUT YOU PLAY IT AGAINST ITSELF...
...WHAT YOU HEAR AND WHAT YOU SEE, Y'SEE, DOC--YOU BOUNCE ONE AGAINST THE NEXT.
THAT'S FUNNY, TO ME. THAT'S FUNNY TO A LOT OF FOLKS.
AND TV GIVES YOU ALL KINDS OF NEW WAYS TO MAKE THOSE JOKES.
I WANT TO MAKE A SHOW YOU HAVE TO WATCH AS MUCH AS YOU HEAR.
IT'D BE SIMPLE. YOU DON'T EVEN NEED...
...I COULD JUST...Y'KNOW, STAND ON A SET OF A STREET CORNER AND, SAY, MEET PEOPLE, NEW PEOPLE, INTERESTING PEOPLE--
SOLD.
HOW ABOUT 15 MINUTES BEFORE THE MORNING LOCAL?
ARE YOU FUCKING WITH ME?
LEMONDE

STAFF LOUNGE
taktaktak taktaktak taktaktaktak taktaktak taktaktak tak

taktak tak taktak
taktaktak taktak

taktaktak DING
taktak taktaktak

FUCKING CHRIST.

SOME-BODY'S WORKING LATE.
taktak tak taktak
taktaktak taktak

FUCK.
WHERE WAS I?
GODDAMNIT.
taktak
tak

con
Mariangela
Melato
e con
Klaus
Kinski
e
Lionel
Stander
ECCO QUI, ECCO QUI E ARRIVATO UN QUADRIMOTORE PIENO DI, PIENO DI INDOVINALO UN PO' DI CHI

SONO TRE CON IL BIANCO MANTELLO D'IMMA-COLATO-
Ahh..
MARIA?

IMPATIENT BOY. I GO AS FAST AS I CAN GO.
I KNOW HOW YOU WANT IT TO BE PERFECT LIKE POSTER, I KNOW, I KNOW.
IT'S NOT *THAT*, DARLING...

...I KNOW IT'S WEDNESDAY NIGHT, BUT WE NEED TO *TALK*.

MARIA, I SPOKE TO MOTHER...
THAT WOMAN, SHE HATE ME.
OH, COME ON NOW, MARIA, IT'S NOT LIKE THAT...
...MOTHER, SHE'S...
...SHE HAS CERTAIN ...OLDER VALUES, SEE, AND...
...IT'S NOT THAT SHE DOESN'T LIKE ITALIANS, MARIA, IT'S THAT SHE--
--WELL, YOU KNOW, LOSING MY BROTHER IN THE WAR AND--
--MOTHER HAS VERY HIGH STANDARDS, YOU SEE. A CERTAIN, I DON'T KNOW, PRECONCEIVED IRISH NOTION--
--OF WHAT KIND OF WOMAN MY WIFE WOULD BE. FROM THE OLD COUNTRY, YOU SEE.
AND, WELL, I GUESS MEETING YOU...SHE ASKED THAT WE JUST...
...NOT CALL IT OFF, NECESSARILY, BUT SLOW DOWN SOME. SHE'D LIKE ME TO MOVE HER INTO MY PLACE FOR A WHILE, TAKE CARE OF HER SOME AND...
...MARIA?
YOU SON OF BITCH--

WHAT'S THAT NOW?
WHAZZAT, LIKE BASEBALL CARDS FOR DIRTY BIRDS?
YOUR DIRTY PICTURES. S'LIKE BASEBALL CARDS.
WELL, DON'T GET *SORE* ABOUT IT.
NO, IT'S NOT THAT, IT'S--
--THIS ONE KIND OF LOOKS LIKE YOU.
I KNEW A DIRTY BIRD A LOT LIKE YOU, ONCE. LIKED TAKIN' PICTURES OF THINGS HE LIKED.
SO, *IS* THIS YOU?
COME FIND OUT.
TELL YOUR GIRLFRIEND NOT TO *WAIT*.

Nng. God.
GOD.

NOT SO NOT SO nnn
NNN
Mmmm?
JESUS.
THE THING, WITH THE HUMMING.
I'LL BE YOUR LITTLE HUMMING-BIRD. Hmmm?

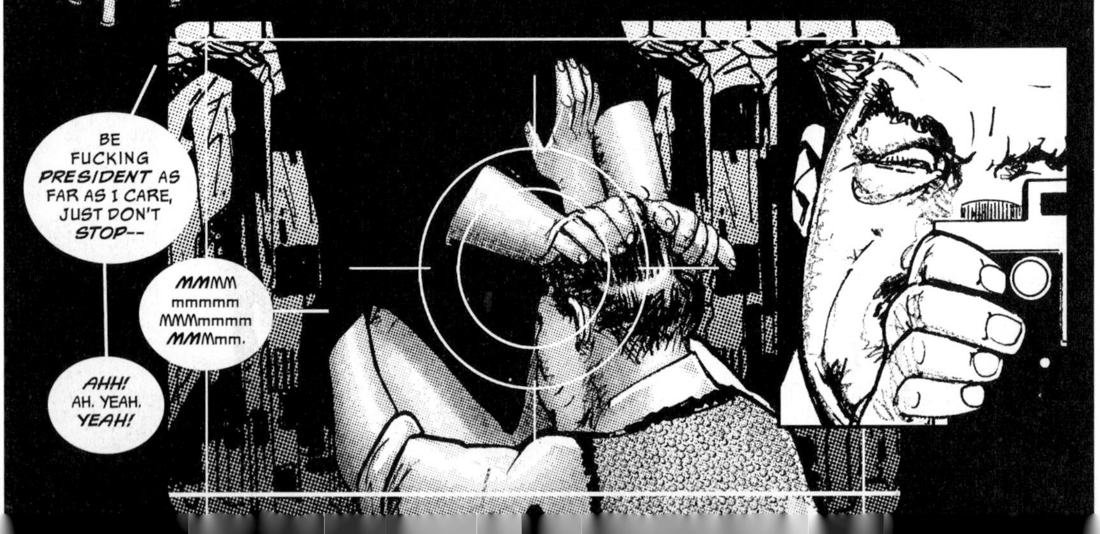

BE FUCKING PRESIDENT AS FAR AS I CARE, JUST DON'T STOP--
MMMM mmmmm MMMmmmm MMMmm.
AHH! AH. YEAH. YEAH!

Air Cooled
AH, C'MON.

THIS GUY AGAIN.
BROTHER, DON'TCHA EVER *LEARN*?

THE LADY ASKED YOU NICE.
AN I *TOLD* YOU NICE, YOU AIN'T TO BE ADMITT-

FUCK YOU!

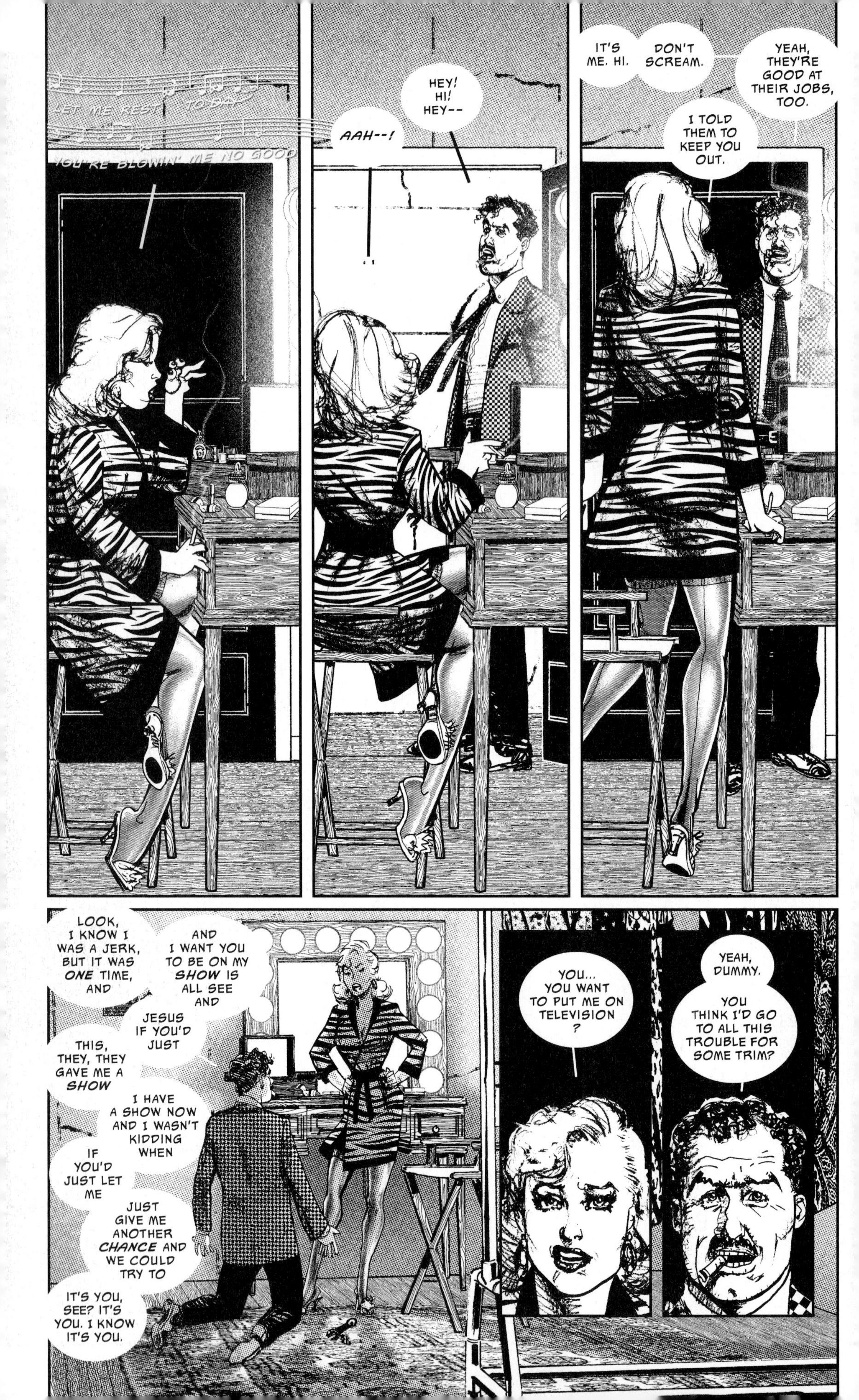
LET ME REST TODAY
YOU'RE BLOWIN' ME NO GOOD
AAH--!
HEY! HI! HEY--
IT'S ME. HI.
DON'T SCREAM.
YEAH, THEY'RE GOOD AT THEIR JOBS, TOO.
I TOLD THEM TO KEEP YOU OUT.
LOOK, I KNOW I WAS A JERK, BUT IT WAS ONE TIME, AND
AND I WANT YOU TO BE ON MY SHOW IS ALL SEE AND
JESUS IF YOU'D JUST
THIS, THEY, THEY GAVE ME A SHOW
I HAVE A SHOW NOW AND I WASN'T KIDDING WHEN
IF YOU'D JUST LET ME
JUST GIVE ME ANOTHER CHANCE AND WE COULD TRY TO
IT'S YOU, SEE? IT'S YOU. I KNOW IT'S YOU.
YOU... YOU WANT TO PUT ME ON TELEVISION?
YEAH, DUMMY.
YOU THINK I'D GO TO ALL THIS TROUBLE FOR SOME TRIM?

SO LOUD OUT THERE I CAN BARELY HEAR M'SELF TALK...
"...OUGHTA HAVE A BIT'A PRIVACY HERE."

WHAT DO YOU WANT TO GIVE ME TO FIND OUT WHAT KIND OF DIRTY BIRD I CAN BE?
YOU KNOW MY FRIEND ANDY JACKSON?

I CAN PARTY A LITTLE WITH PRESIDENT JACKSON, BABY, SURE.
WHAT ABOUT YOUR PHOTOGRAPHER FRIEND? DID HE PAY YOU, TOO?

EVERY-BODY PAYS EVENTUALLY, SWEET-HEART.
"EVERYBODY."

OMAHA?
OKLAHOMA.
OKLAHOMA?
YEAH, OKLAHOMA.
OKAY, THEN FINE, SO SHE WENT BACK TO OKLA--
EXCUSE ME?
OKLAHOMA. GREAT, GOT IT.
THANK YOU FOR YOUR TIME.
GOTTA MAKE A PHONE CALL.

Ahh--
Duh.
DON'T.
DON'T STOP.
AHHH--

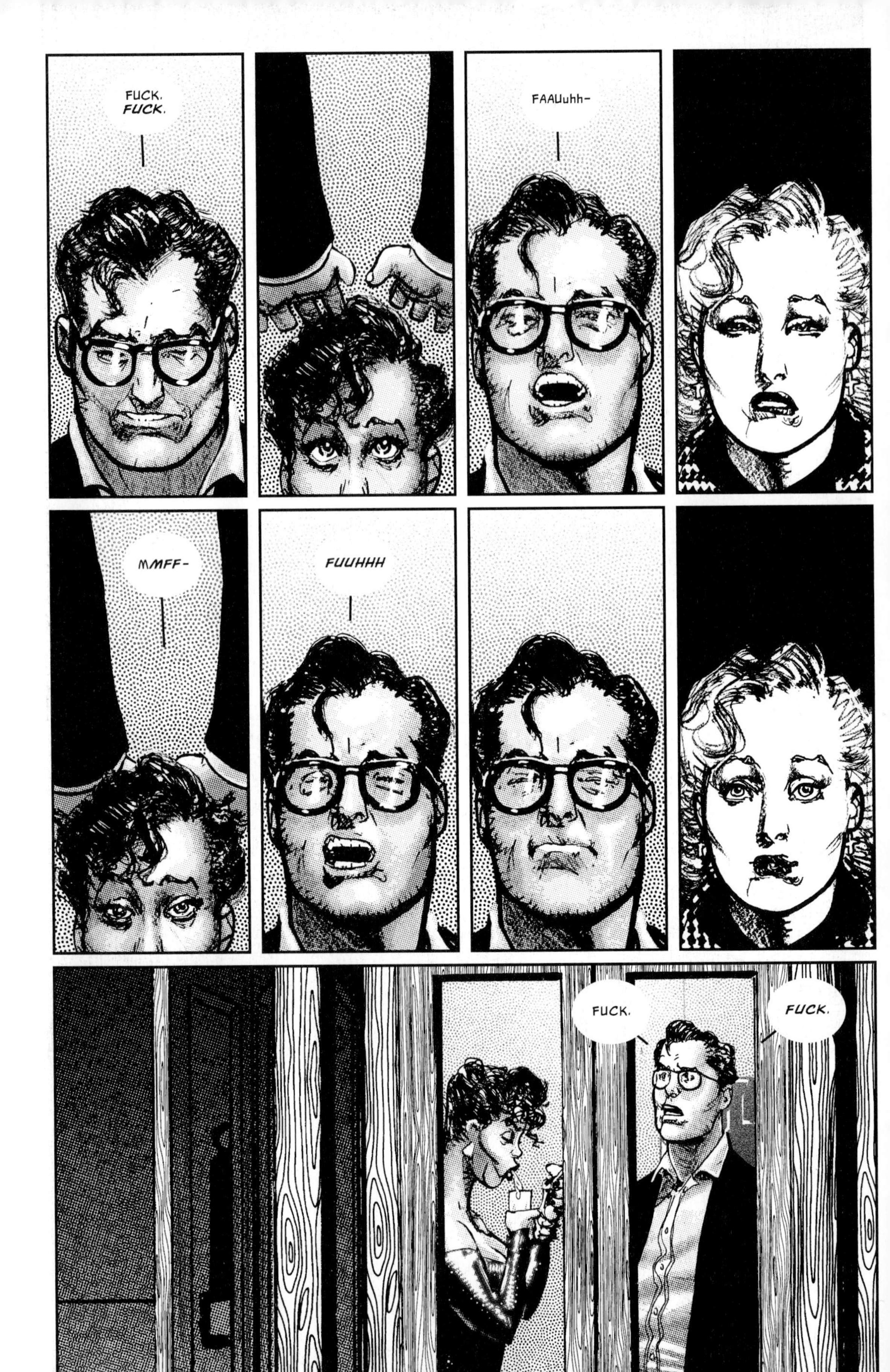
FUCK.
FUCK.
FAAUuhh-
MMFF-
FUUHHH
FUCK.
FUCK.

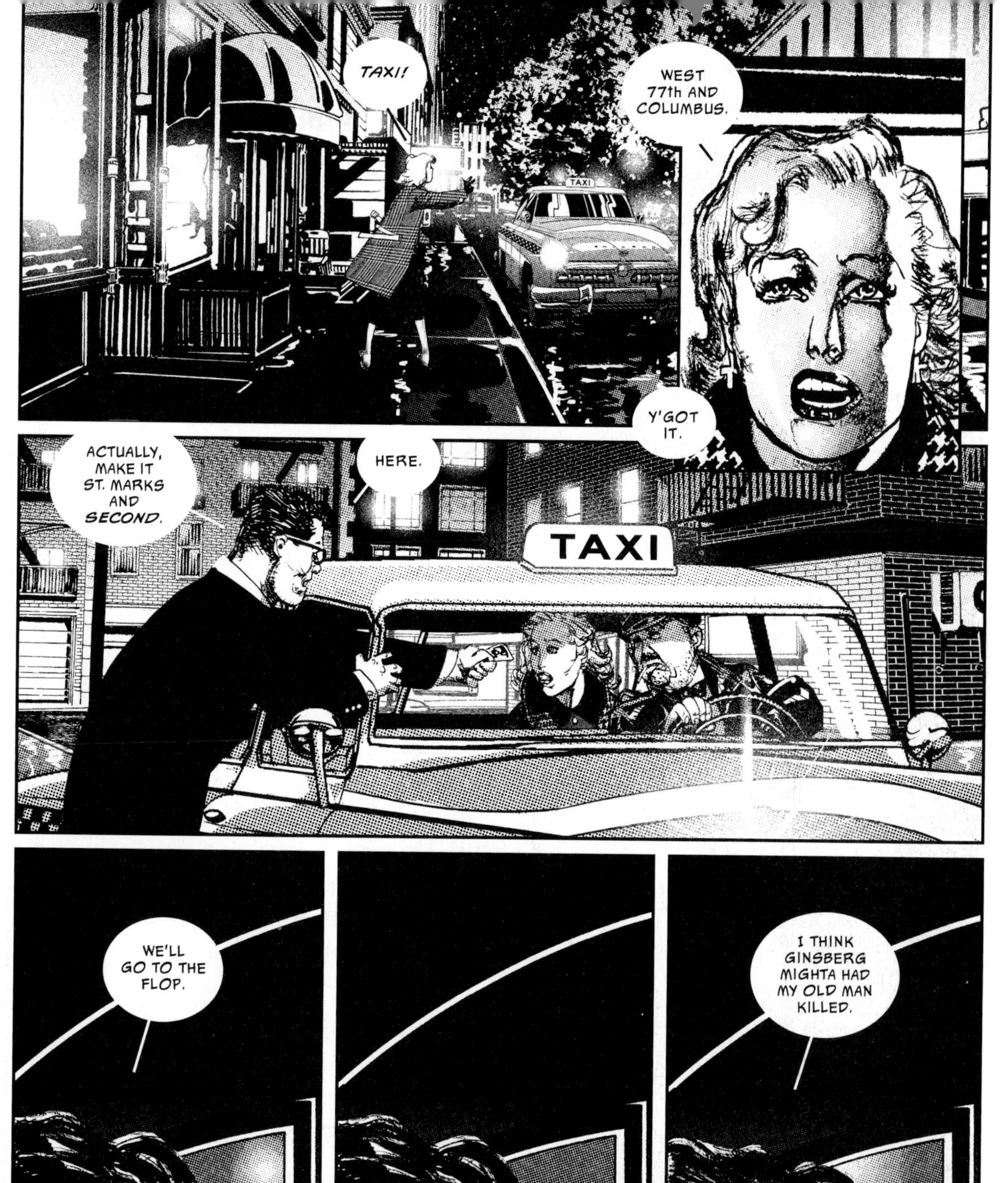
TAXI!
WEST 77th AND COLUMBUS.
Y'GOT IT.
ACTUALLY, MAKE IT ST. MARKS AND *SECOND*.
HERE.
TAXI

WE'LL GO TO THE FLOP.

I THINK GINSBERG MIGHTA HAD MY OLD MAN KILLED.

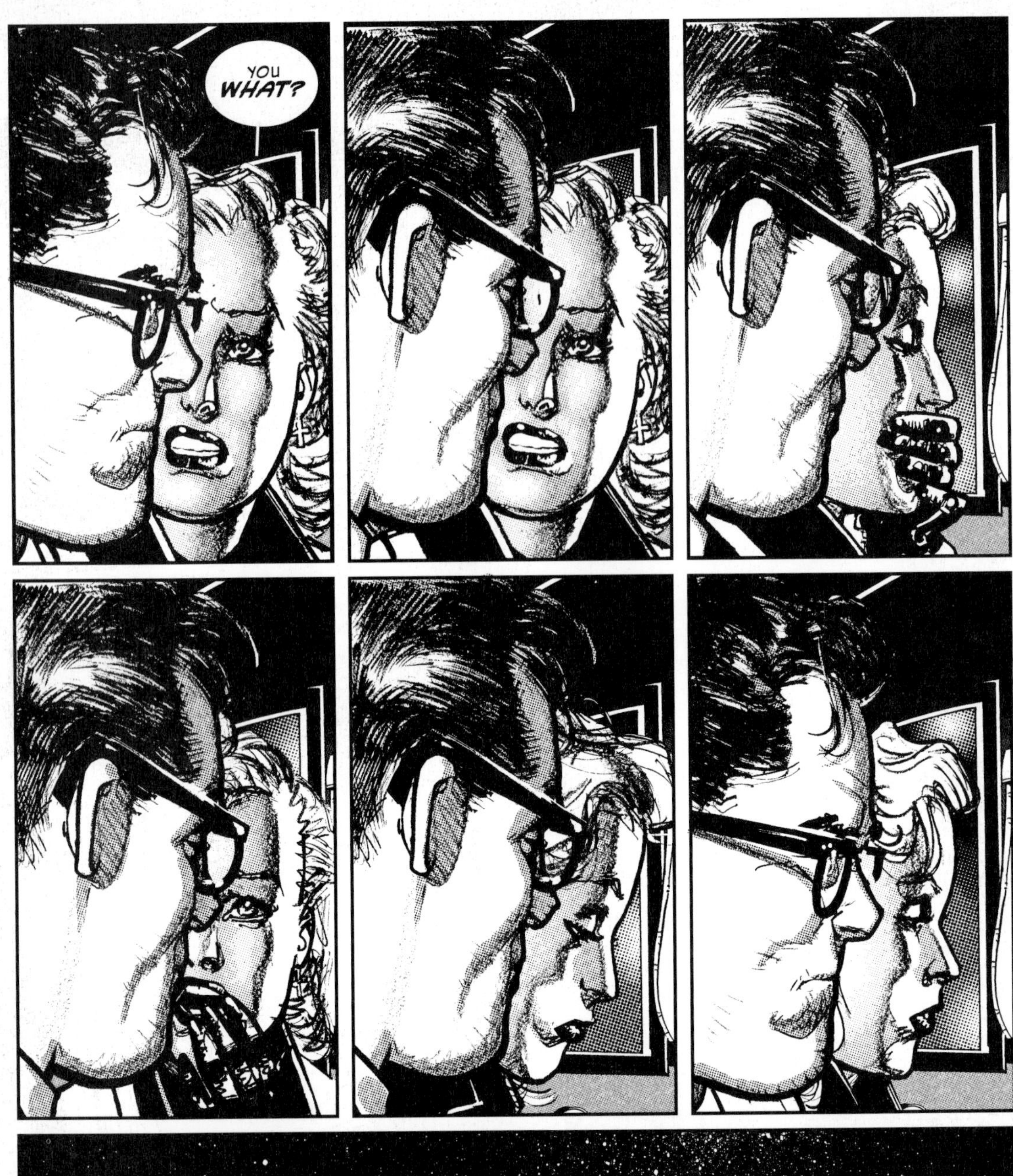
YOU WHAT?

EXTRAS

Various pieces of art, design, and narrative work produced for the SATELLITE SAM series follow; produced for the monthly comic, this work served purposes that, when the story itself came together as a collection, didn't necessarily feel proper when assembled chronologically. That said, we all LIKE the work that follows and wanted it represented here, but it didn't make sense to reprint the collection in the same format as the serial issues.

THE CAST PAGES felt necessary due to the sprawling nature of the ensemble and the aggressive manner with which we introduced it; once Howard and I realized we wanted to keep doing SAM for as long as they'll let us, we found ourselves free to explore who these people are and how they got to LeMonde, and our one-man show became an ensemble with a strong lead. A little monthly reminder felt wise; I always know I need to go back and rewrite when I can't sum one of 'em up this tightly. As you have hopefully read this in a shorter time than the 6 months during which we originally published, you, hopefully, have less need for this every 20 pages or so.

THE COVERS contain an array of where we went and where we're going by way of tantalizing advertisement, we hope. Abnormal interest in our first issue from retailers and readers meant the first issue came in a variety of covers. After the spread sorry cover of issue five, we've teased here the subsequent five covers that will span the contents of our next collection, SATELLITE SAM AND THE SNUFF-FUCK KINESCOPE.

CHAYKIN gives great interview. Dig up Costello's HOWARD CHAYKIN: CONVERSATIONS to read the master at work. My favorite thing about working on SAM has been the excuse it gives me to *bug Chaykin all the time* about literally any damn thing in my sad little head. As the man was alive in New York at the time of our story and a well-documented television baby, I wanted to ask him about that era...this is the kind of stuff that I know must annoy the shit out of him and yet I ask anyway. You might not learn anything, but I hope just some of the joy I feel working with him shines through. I wrote this book for him. I write this book because of him. Howard? You're a prince among men and a king among princes.

MICHAEL WHITE: shell-shocked engineer, alcoholic, son of the late CARLYLE, a.k.a. SATELLITE SAM.
Dr. JOSEPH GINSBERG: founder and owner of the failing LeMONDE TELEVISION NETWORK, inventor, and prick.
KARA KELLY: SATELLITE SAM'S ebullient co-star, evangelical, most-masturbated-to girl on the payroll.
HAMILTON STANHOPE: SATELLITE SAM co-star, raging blunderbuss, practiced devourer of catering and scenery.
CLINT HAYGOOD: SATELLITE SAM co-star, giftless little asshole, maddeningly popular sidekick.
MARIANGELA MELATO: SATELLITE SAM co-star, European exotic, first role in now-forgotten Italian royalist propaganda, or a smoker. Probably a smoker.
DICK DANNING: director and producer of SATELLITE SAM. Two moves ahead, three if he has enough cameras.
GUY ROTH: writer and primary apologist of SATELLITE SAM. Claims to have a novel, but doesn't. Claims to have a girlfriend, but doesn't.
EUGENE FORD: video shader at LeMONDE, tinkerer. Inveterate smartass and incorrigible hound.
LIBBY MEYERS: assistant director, continuity, and glue that holds together all things SATELLITE SAM.

Cast page from SATELLITE SAM #2

MICHAEL WHITE:
Drunk, shell-shocked and standing in as the star of SATELLITE SAM in his late father's stead.

KARA KELLY:
Evangelical on the one hand, SATELLITE SAM dream girl to millions of prepubescent boys on the other.

Dr. JOSEPH GINSBERG:
LeMONDE TELEVISION NETWORK president, CEO, primary inventor, visionary, and all-around asshole.

MADELINE GINSBERG:
Old money. The asshole's wife. Not an insult -- that's her self- image.

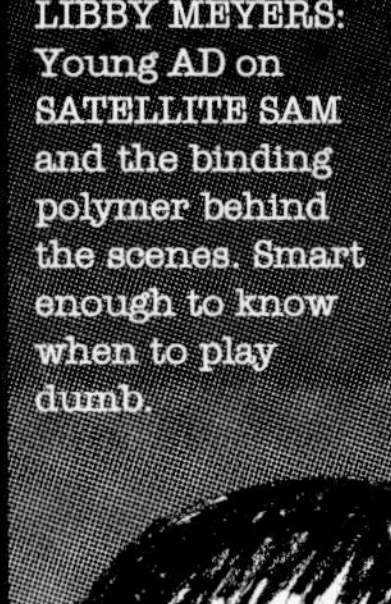

LIBBY MEYERS:
Young AD on SATELLITE SAM and the binding polymer behind the scenes. Smart enough to know when to play dumb.

MARIANGELA MELATO:
SATELLITE SAM import star and wellspring of smoldering post-Fascist sensuality.

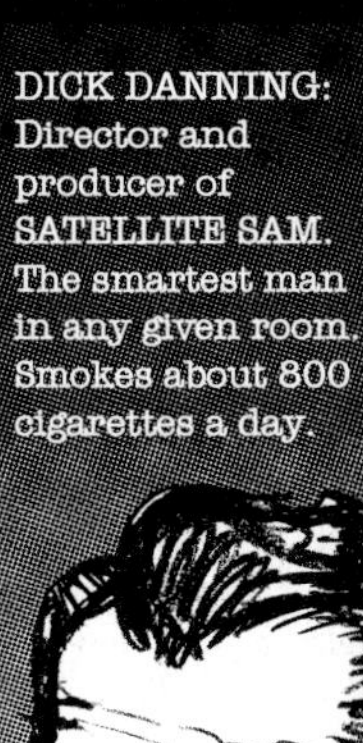

DICK DANNING:
Director and producer of SATELLITE SAM. The smartest man in any given room. Smokes about 800 cigarettes a day.

IKE EIGER:
Technical Director at LeMONDE. Radio lifer now in television. Too damn old for the cutting edge of something so new.

EUGENE FORD:
Video shader at LeMONDE; tinkerer. Hopelessly sarcastic prick able to see the future of television like almost no one else.

EVE ECHOL:
Jazz club singer. Small-room sizzle epitomized. Charming naivete allows her belief voice is her true calling card.

Cast page from SATELLITE SAM #3

MICHAEL WHITE:
The son of the late Carlyle White, creator of SATELLITE SAM and secret sex fiend. Dry drunk, shell-shocked, and an overnight TV star with a great big hole in his middle.

KARA KELLY: TV's first girl for Christ, SATELLITE SAM co-star, drawn to help Michael out of love and respect for his late father--the guy who saved her life and got her out of the gutter.

MARIA MELATO:
Ingénue émigré from Fascist Italy now chewing the silver-painted scenery with the rest of the gang on SATELLITE SAM.

DICK DANNING:
If television could be said to have a veteran director in these early days, it'd be him.

EUGENE FORD:
TV tech and wannabe director. Tinkerer, thinker, experimenter. Usually a girl-hound, but he's caught whiff of one that's shutting him out and he can't get her out of his head.

GUY ROTH:
Writer "writing" SATELLITE SAM while being harassed by its lesser cast into expanding their parts to fill Michael's void.

DOCTOR JOSEPH GINSBERG:
President, founder and CEO of the LeMONDE network, waiting for the FCC to grant him and his network its blessing to grow.

MADELINE GINSBERG:
Old-money wife and the woman behind the man behind LeMONDE. Also the woman on top of the man on top of the FCC obstructing LeMONDE. Tricky.

HAMILTON STANHOPE:
Hack actor giggled off Broadway and into millions of homes, 15 inches at a time.

LIBBY MEYERS:
Girl Friday on SATELLITE SAM dealing with as many pieces of Carlyle White's absence as his son. And she's starting to ask questions...

Cast page from SATELLITE SAM #4

MICHAEL WHITE: Former engineer and nascent TV star of SATELLITE SAM, on the prowl for women that knew his father, on the run from the bottle.

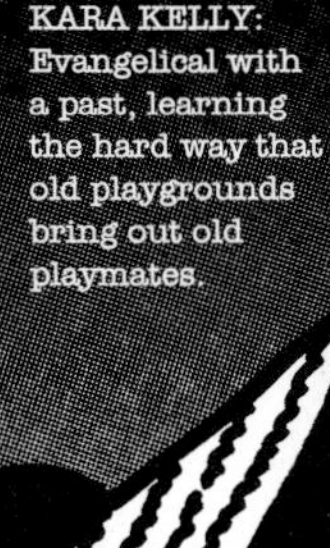

KARA KELLY: Evangelical with a past, learning the hard way that old playgrounds bring out old playmates.

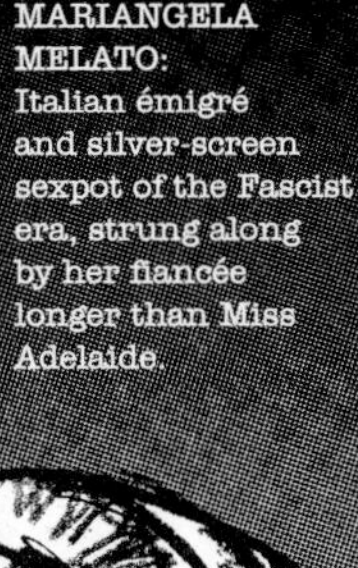

MARIANGELA MELATO: Italian émigré and silver-screen sexpot of the Fascist era, strung along by her fiancée longer than Miss Adelaide.

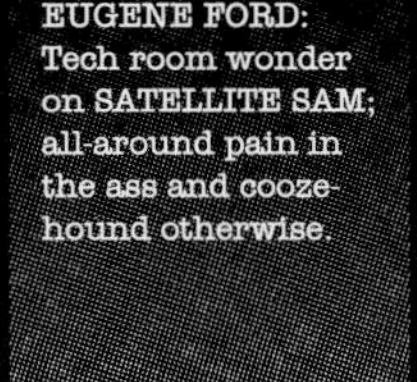

EUGENE FORD: Tech room wonder on SATELLITE SAM; all-around pain in the ass and cooze-hound otherwise.

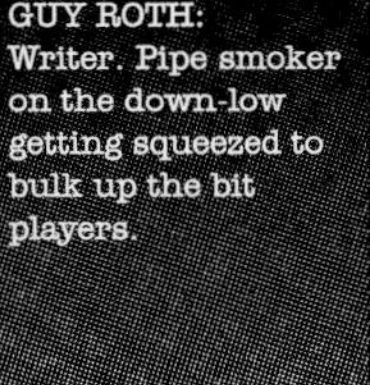

GUY ROTH: Writer. Pipe smoker on the down-low getting squeezed to bulk up the bit players.

Dr. JOSEPH GINSBERG: President of the LeMONDE NETWORK; willing to go to extraordinary lengths to ensure its survival.

MADDIE GINSBERG: The good wife of the good doctor, and just in it for the ride.

HAMILTON STANHOPE: Odious screen presence and all-around-noxious-bag-of-fuck co-star on SATELLITE SAM.

EVE ECHOL: Middling singer on the middle rung of the middle ladder, on Gene's radar and shutting him down hard.

WILSON "Reb" KARNES: Running and fucking his way from New York and the FCC all the way to Washington, DC.

Cast page from SATELLITE SAM #5

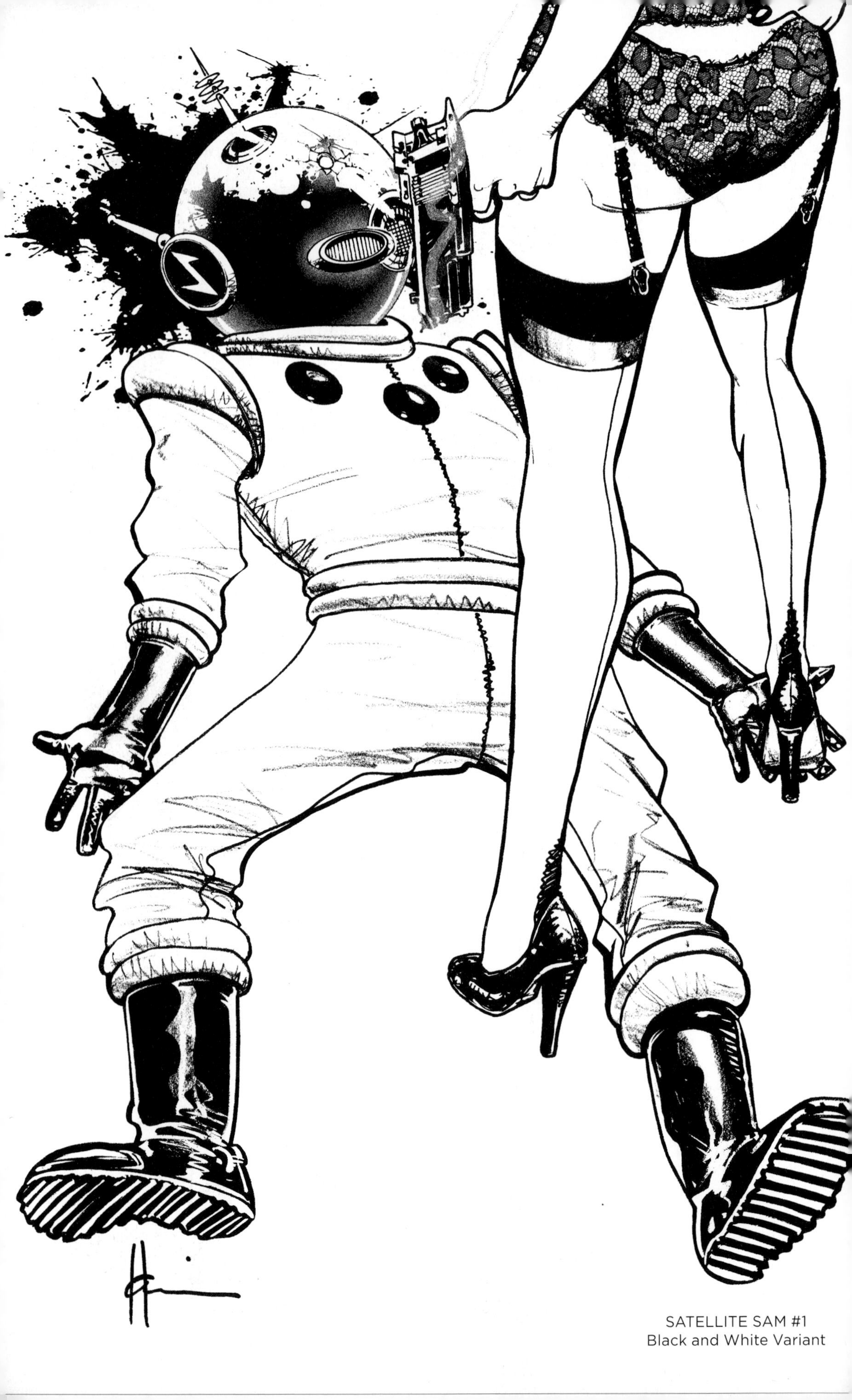

SATELLITE SAM #1
Black and White Variant

SATELLITE SAM #1
Mile High Comics
Variant

SATELLITE SAM
SATELLITE SAM #1
Midtown Comics
Black and White
Variant

SATELLITE SAM
SATELLITE SAM
SATELLITE SAM
SATELLITE SAM
SATELLITE SAM
SATELLITE SAM
SATELLITE SAM #1
Midtown Comics
Variant

SATELLITE SAM #1
Image Expo Variant

SATELLITE SAM #1
2nd Printing Cover

SATELLITE SAM #1

SATELLITE SAM #2

SATELLITE SAM #3

SATELLITE SAM #4

SATELLITE SAM #5

Cover from the upcoming
SATELLITE SAM #6

Cover from the upcoming
SATELLITE SAM #7

Cover from the upcoming
SATELLITE SAM #8

Cover from the upcoming
SATELLITE SAM #9

Cover from the upcoming
SATELLITE SAM #10

SATELLITE SAM

SAMSKRIT

BEHIND THE SCENES WITH FRACTION & CHAYKIN

MF Howard, do you remember the world before television? Were you old enough to remember when TV entered your landscape?

HVC Matt, I don't. Frankly, television is so much a part of my childhood that, I'm ashamed to admit, there might be more defining moments that are video based than, say, family derived.

My grandmother owned a DUMONT, where I discovered my first two obsessions, HOWDY DOODY and HOPALONG CASSIDY. I was also driven out of the living room in shrieking terror by a show entitled THE MAGIC CLOWN, whose makeup was the perfect reflection of Lon Chaney's quote, "Even a clown is frightening in the moonlight."

My father brought a used ZENITH to our apartment in Brooklyn when I was five, and I remember catching the CISCO KID halfway through an episode within minutes of its warmup.

I love television, and have from word one.

MF Were you early adopters? How soon did your family have a set compared to your neighbors? One of my favorite bits of color I've found in researching the early years was the phenomenon of neighbors from all around coming to one family's house at prime time to watch whatever was on—paint drying, a sermon, Milton Berle...

HVC That sort of thing predates my birth and childhood by a couple of years, certainly in Brooklyn and other urban areas.

By the time I was completely and totally addicted to the tube, say, 1955, everyone had a set—they were as ubiquitous as refrigerators. Although radio drama lived on into the early 1960s, I was utterly unaware of it.

MF Were you always aware you were going to be some kind of artist and storyteller? What was your artistic temperament as a kid? And was there any inkling when watching HOWDY DOODY of the kind of manic hijinks as documented in Stephen Davis' "Say Kids! What Time Is It?" or was that all behind the scenes and obscured?

HVC As I've documented elsewhere, I inherited a refrigerator box half filled with comics—comics of every genre—just after I turned four. I fell in love with comics immediately—and within a year, I was reading on a fourth grade level.

Doing comics was all I ever wanted to do. In lieu of talent or ability, I had hunger and desire—sensibilities that sustain me, professionally at the very least, to this day.

All I knew about all those backstage hijinks was sneaking a read of Judy Tyler's obit in the New York Daily Mirror, the sleaziest of the New York tabloids of the day.

MF Do you have a recollection of television's dramatic possibilities penetrating your radar?

HVC Not even a little. I was a comics guy. Television was simply something I loved, almost uncritically. The closest I ever came to that sort of thing was the Ernie Kovacs morning show, on ABC, which was clearly a bunch of nuts having a good time. This same attitude informed the Steve Allen show of the early '60s, on which Allen—a huge influence on everything comic on TV today, who pissed away his legacy by becoming a tiresome asshole late in life—behaved recklessly, pushing the envelope

But of course, all this was later. For me, back in my childhood, my tastes were defined by THE LONE RANGER, ROY ROGERS AND DALE EVANS, GENE AUTRY, THE MICKEY MOUSE CLUB, and of course Xavier Cugat and his then-consort, Abbe Lane—my first serious crush.

MF Did you ever see any TV be made live? Were you ever part of a studio audience?

HVC Despite the fact that my childhood was peppered with broken promises of a visit to the peanut gallery on HOWDY DOODY, or the unnamed audience on THE PINKY LEE SHOW, and my stoned-out inability to get my shit together to hit the MD TELETHON, my only experience with live TV was SATURDAY NIGHT LIVE in the late seventies.

MF Did any of the sci-fi serials like "Satellite Sam" hit you at all? When we were putting the book together we spent a slab of time at the Paley Center in Manhattan together watching old shows and you were struck by the quality and craft in contrast to your memory...

HVC I was a huge fan of CAPTAIN VIDEO and SCIENCE FICTION THEATER with TRUMAN BRADLEY, whoever the fuck he was. I also watched ROCKY JONES, SPACE RANGER and CAPTAIN MIDNIGHT, which lost its license in reruns, and was retitled JET JACKSON. His lips said "CAPTAIN MIDNIGHT,' but his voice said "JET JACKSON."

I have no recollection of seeing SPACE PATROL, so I was impressed by the line one might draw from it to STAR TREK. I might add, even then I knew CAPTAIN VIDEO was a ridiculously cheap piece of shit.

MF It's insane to think they were putting shows like SPACE PATROL on daily. I think that was part of what got me thinking about SATELLITE SAM and "Satellite Sam," if that makes sense. This insane and rapid "let's put on a show" energy combined with rudimentary special effects and elaborate costumes and everything else... EVERY DAY. The adrenaline alone must've aged all involved a good twenty years.

So when you transitioned into television writing, did you find your time in comics helped or hurt or... what was it like? As serial narratives sometimes I think comics and television might have more in common as a storytelling form than comics and film but, then again, comics don't have the levels of bullshit TV has to navigate. Looking back on it, what was your time making TV like?

HVC It's important to remember that the audience was mostly kids, and of course the occasional unemployed horndog getting off on the starlets. I had a cousin with serious obsession with Mary Hartline, the majorette on SUPER CIRCUS, but that's another story...

And recall as well that these were radio veterans alongside ignorant newcomers, who had no real model from which to work—so the insanity you describe was likely more the norm than you can imagine. Bear in mind the work ethic of the 1950s derived from a mindset that had just survived a depression and a world war—these guys were no strangers to desperation, and would likely hold on to anything, and put up with any demand, in order to never face the wolf of their younger years again.

My first hour of television was the most expensive hour ever produced for CBS. I learned rapidly from there how to economize, so that by my second year, I was frequently the go-to guy for bottle shows—that anathema of old time TV, when the money was gone, so an episode that never left the standing sets was needed—a step before the clip show. Be grateful for modern TV—these things truly sucked.

I've come to believe my television writing experience impacted on my comics writing in a much deeper way than the reverse. We've discussed my graphics process—which I won't go into here, because it's nobody's business—but much of that thinking derives from television's production demands.

And yes, I wholeheartedly agree that writing for television and writing for comics have more in common than, say, film and comics.

I might add that the first half of my television career was spent working for a couple of the best guys I've ever known, who were doomed from word one, by a combination of the lack of killer instinct, as well as a complete misunderstanding of what they were competing with.

The second half of that career was in the service of some of the worst shitweasel scumbag lowlifes who ever walked the earth, upon whom I wished ass cancer.

That second bunch is far more the norm.

MF So now then, on the other side of that time, and you're back in comics and now we're DOING a comic about TV, do you find your time in that industry influences SATELLITE SAM, beyond your graphics process?

HVC Actually, I'm far more informed by my experience watching—make that growing up with—television. My time spent in TV was in the ass end—making junk. As I've said any number of times, maybe even here already, I never worked on a show I'd watch. None of this obviates my gratitude for the career I had.

I will say that, from a technical production standpoint, my experience as a producer has had an odd and difficult-to-explain effect on my approach to the actual production of comic art. I'll say no more than that, as I'm fully aware of the comics audience's desperate need to know how it's done—followed by disappointment with the talent once that knowledge is acquired.

MF Girls keep being mentioned here — first crushes and such. So much of your work has a current of... Of, what, desire, hunger, call it what you will, running through it; as you grew up, as more women crossed your radar, and the comics and art making-slash-storytelling didn't go away, did television feed you, did television feed THAT for you, the way it did me? I remember seeing some kind of Lady Godiva recreation on fucking FANTASY ISLAND far too young and forever after thinking on some level TV could and would summon the things you wanted to look at if you just looked long enough...

HVC An unqualified yes. From the moment I saw Abbe Lane—a nice Jewish girl, I learned years later, strutting her stuff with Xavier Cugat when I was five—up to and including seeing a woman whose name I've long forgotten with whom I had a one-night stand showing up on Al Goldstein's MIDNIGHT BLUE, doing a submissive and exhibitionistic dance/crawl across a floor, TV has had a huge impact on me, both romantically and erotically.

As I've stated above, I spent years loving television nearly uncritically—and I recall with enormous fondness two Mexican cantadoras of the '70s, Iris Chacon and Olga Breeskin, busty blondes who sang in Spanish, dressed in gowns and halters held in place by hope and trickery.

And don't get me started with Christina Hendricks.

MF What is it about "The Fifties" (as generic a term as that is) that provokes the nostalgia that it does? And what is it about nostalgia that whitewashes all the sin and kink and character away? It struck me, again and again and again as I read up on the era, that the kind of scandal and voracious depravity we for whatever reason associate with more modern times were just as prevalent, if not more so, in the fifties. Is it as simple as every generation thinking it was the one that discovered sex? Have we mistaken the antiseptic airwaves for actual memories?

HVC One of the defining images of the 1950s has to be those black bars that magazines, particularly those dealing in a kind of bait and switch titillation, like CONFIDENTIAL and its many imitators, ran over the eyes of men and women "caught" in compromising situations. Fat lot of good those black bars did—but they were a statement—futile, certainly—about a desire to misbehave in private.

I think we make those associations you mention primarily due to a willing sacrifice of that privacy, a misbegotten take on the 1960s' "let it all hang out." Before people found they could achieve celebrity, or notoriety, or whatever, by airing their dirty laundry in public, there was an unspoken rule, perhaps hypocritical, that public and private behavior were separate entities.

In many if not most cases, this was a perfectly justified reaction to the law. Remember, oral sex was illegal in the US—for married couples. Forget about extramarital sex, or homosexuality.

I also remain convinced that the public masks of the 1950s were a perhaps indirect result of the depression and the war—that these people had had enough shit in their lives, and were keeping their heads down to avoid what seemed like the next onslaught from hell.

And yes—media of the time told a series of lies so effectively that I spend hours countermanding assumptions about those days with my children and grandchildren.

ALSO AVAILABLE

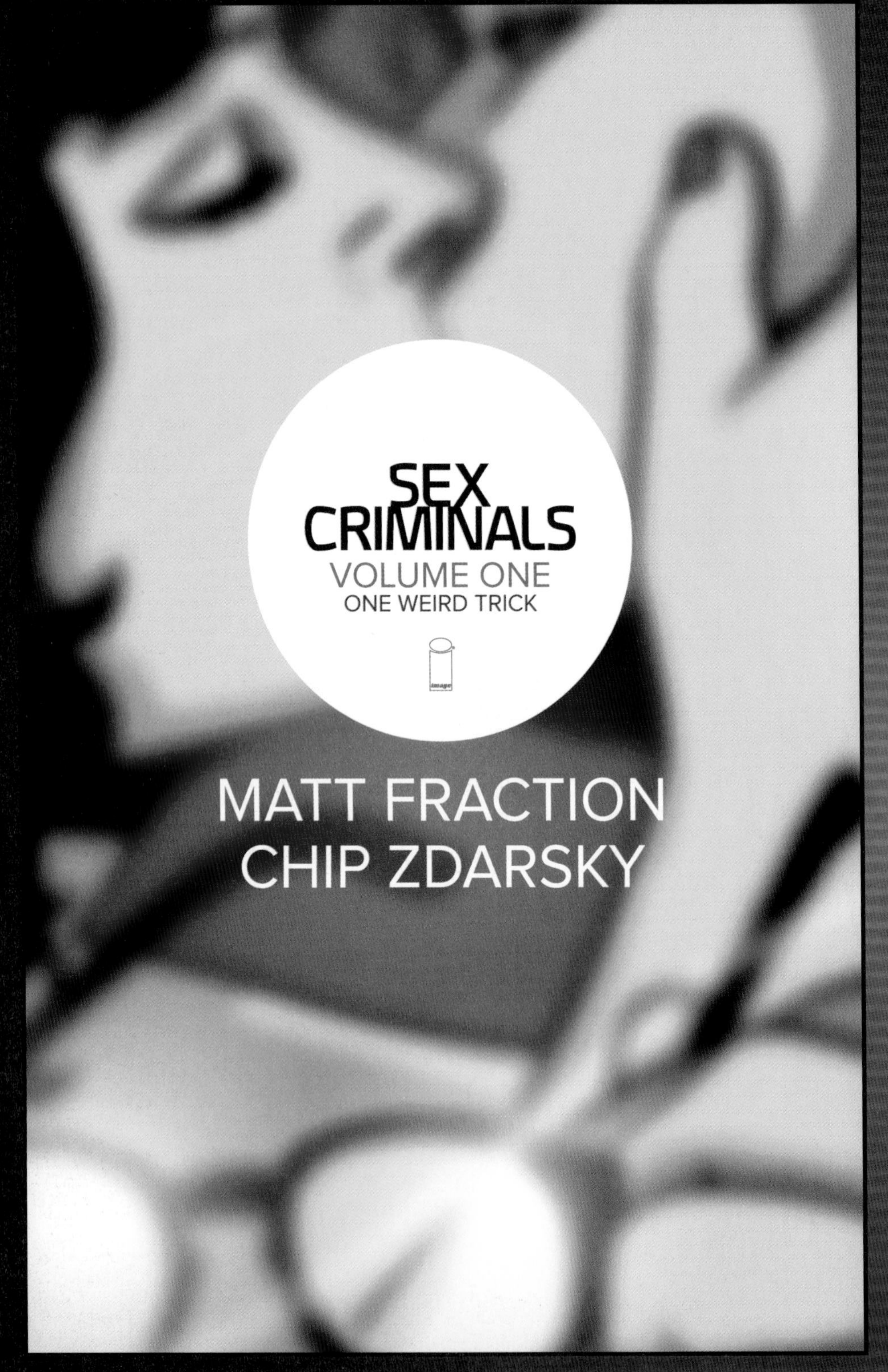

Suzie's just a regular gal with an irregular gift: when she has sex, she stops time. One day she meets Jon and it turns out he has the same ability. And sooner or later they get around to using their gifts to do what we'd ALL do: rob a couple banks. A bawdy and brazen sex comedy for comics begins here!

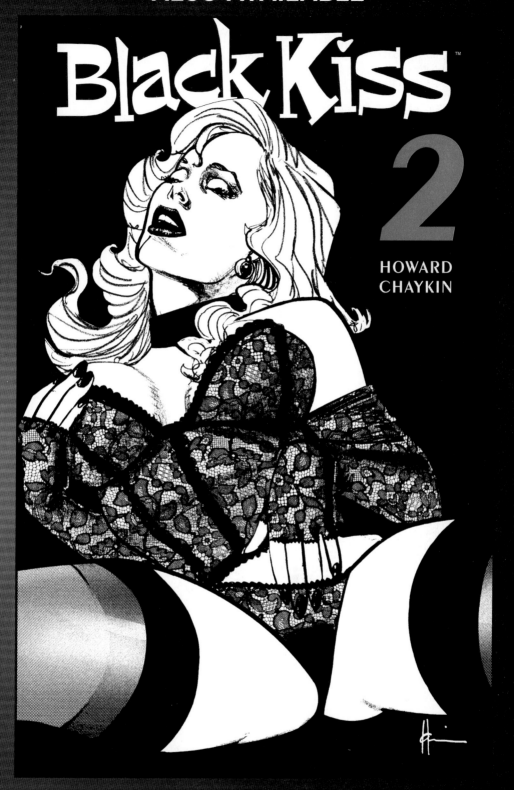

ALSO AVAILABLE

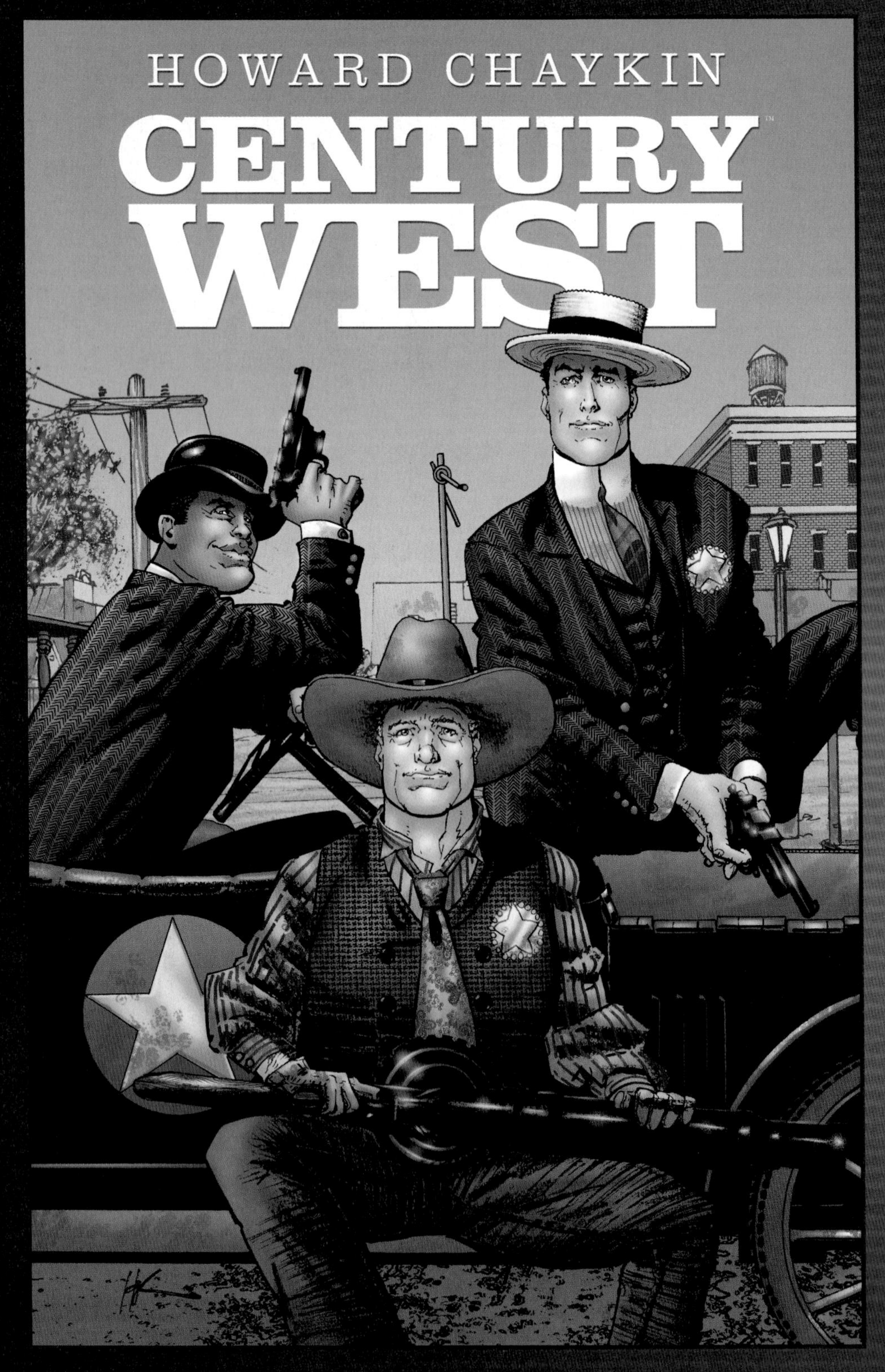

Century, Texas used to be a sleepy little burg, barely a whistlestop between nowhere and the great beyond... until the 20th Century arrived with a bang, bringing with it automobiles, aeroplanes, telephones, paved streets... and, of course, the movies. Howard Chaykin tells the colorful story of the American West, transformed from frontier to legend, and how the American dream became a modern myth.

WILL RETURN IN

VOLUME TWO:
SATELLITE SAM AND THE SNUFF-FUCK KINESCOPE

SATELLITE SAM, VOL 1: THE LONESOME DEATH OF SATELLITE SAM. First printing. March 2014. Published by Image Comics, Inc. Office of publication: 2001 Center Street, Sixth Floor, Berkeley, CA 94704. Contains material originally published as Satellite Sam #1-5. Printed in the USA. For information regarding the CPSIA on this printed material call: 203-595-3636 and provide reference # RICH-541742. For international rights, contact: foreignlicensing@imagecomics.com. ISBN: 978-1-60706-852-5